EDITORIAL REVIEW

Thor's Dragon Rider
Book Four

Hoodwinked

"Kara and Elan are back in Hoodwinked, the next chapter in their ongoing quest to get back in the gods' good graces and back to their home in Asgard. The land of the elves seems peaceful and inviting, but Loki is still free, and Kara is well aware that he could be impersonating nearly anyone or anything! An exciting addition to the series." Kelly R., Line Editor, Red Adept Editing

NORSE DRAGON BOOKS

Valkyrie Academy Dragon Alliance Series

Marked Prequel

Chosen

Vanished

Scorned

Inflicted

Empowered

Ambushed

Warned

Abducted

Besieged

Deceived

Thor's Dragon Rider Series

Safeguard

Pursuit

Entrapment

Hoodwinked

More To Come

Hoodwinked

Ebook first published in USA in January 2021 by Cosy Burrow Books

Ebook first published in Great Britain in January 2021 by Cosy Burrow Books

www.katrinacopebooks.com

Text Copyright © 2020 by Katrina Cope

Cover Design Copyright © art4artists.com.au

Published by Cosy Burrow Books

ISBN: 978-0-6450874-0-6

❀ Created with Vellum

To my readers - this is for you.
The world is a crazy place. Where better to escape than a
high fantasy story?

BLURB

Hunted, banished, and desperate to rectify her errors.

The pressure is real. Capture the weaselly god, Loki, and his children will unleash their vengeance. Leave him free, and he will weave his deception with dire consequences. With banishment added to the mix, the only way to rectify the situation is to recapture Loki. It's a demand Kara must accept.

Unable to return to Asgard, Kara is sent to the peaceful realm of Alfheim to enhance her light magic. Once again, trouble seems to find her, obstructing her path with dubious characters and smashing her judgment of who can be trusted.

The race is on to enhance her magic and capture Loki before he deceives her again. If she doesn't, her exile will last forever.

Chapter One

"Welcome." A young woman with pointed ears and long blond hair cascading to her waist smiles at me, her blue eyes and creaseless face radiating tenderness. She lifts a flower lei and loops it over my head.

Apprehension prickles my skin as many elves approach in pastel-hued tunics and long, flowing gowns—the placidness and peace ring alarm bells in my head. People can't be this tranquil all the time, and this seems like a front. The dirt-crusted sweat at the back of my leather fighting uniform crackles when the blond-haired female elf straightens the lei and pulls at the seams around the neck.

Another young female with pale, freckled skin and auburn hair to the middle of her back loops another flowered lei around Eir's neck. Dried leaves snap under the elf's sandals, which are bridged with a strap of soft-colored flowers.

My feet feel burdened by lead, my boots firmly rooted as I stare at the light elf fondling me. Her eyes are a soft lilac, the blond eyelashes incredibly long, and a golden belt tied around the waist of her long flowing white gown covers her sensuous curves. Golden straps secure her loose-fitting sleeves to her upper arms, and gold trims the plunging neckline. Flowered straps anchored beside the first toe hold her sandals in place also.

After having spent so much time in the harsh realm of Muspelheim, I find my senses on full alert, fired up and ready to pick up any malice from these two females or any of the elves semicircled behind them. Except, I can't find any. I sense no hint of any kind that I'm not welcome. That's a hard feeling to process. All the other realms that I've been to always held something aggressive, making the experience dangerous. Yet as I stare into this elf's peaceful lilac eyes, I find it discomfiting in the opposite way. They all seem too welcoming, which raises my suspicions.

Large palms surround us, their greenery mixed with cordylines displaying their variety of colors and textures, along with lush tropical bushes. Flowers speckle the colorful display bordering the semicircle of elves. Not far through the trees, a waterfall cascades into a small stream that gurgles over some rocks. Although the beauty is beckoning to me, I don't let my sight waver from the welcoming elves in front of me. Whether the warning bells chiming inside are warranted or not, I can't quiet them.

Is it me, or are these elves just way too friendly? Elan's voice pierces my thoughts, bringing a smidgen of comfort knowing I'm not alone in my anxiety.

Not wanting to alert the elves that we don't trust them, I nod silently.

Naga thinks it's nice. Naga likes these elves. They are peaceful, and their eyes are friendly. In the corner of my eye, Naga's pale blue forms sits, and he pushes back on his front legs, tilting his head to one side. His big blue eyes survey the small gathering of elves as though he's met a group of new friends.

"Thank you so much." Eir's voice cracks my thoughts and breaks the dragon's conversation. With a face full of gratitude, she clasps the hand of the freckled-faced elf. "It's so nice to be welcomed in your realm. I look forward to getting to know you."

Nothing betrays the sarcasm or aggression on Eir's face I'd expect from Hildr. I should have known the elves' peaceful ways would resonate with her.

Like the blonde, the redhead also wears a long, flowing white gown that drifts around her legs as she dips elegantly into a slight curtsy and inclines her head. With wide eyes and a heart full of skepticism, I openly study Eir, stunned as she tilts her head to the elf imitating her actions.

Elan's voice breaks my thoughts, pulling me from my stupor. *Why don't you imitate Eir? I think it's best if we play along until we work out what's going on.* Her mindspeak is a rushed hush and pulls at my emotional discomfort as I quickly assess the situation. Mentally, I feel gently pushed by Elan's wings toward the female elf in front of me, and I want to dig in my heels.

I blink twice rapidly then stare at the sensuous blond woman. "Oh… um… yes. Thank you very much for your welcome. Er… it's a pleasant change from where I've just come from."

The female elf in front of me curtsies, precisely as the auburn elf had, her blue eyes not leaving mine as I incline my head, imitating Eir's response. Elan is correct—not knowing what the customs are here, I should imitate their actions and respect them and their traditions.

Ooh! Very good imitation! It looks like they've accepted your response favorably. Hopefully, all is as it seems, and nothing sinister lies underneath, Elan says.

Naga thinks all is good. A strange and rare kind of annoyance laces Naga's voice. *Naga likes a friendly reception, and not everyone is out to cause trouble.*

"Thank you, ladies." Freyr's smooth, charming

voice, laced with sensuality, sounds from over our shoulders. He cuts between us and places a gentle hand on each woman's arm.

Girly giggles push aside any sign of womanhood as the two beautiful elves cave toward the god, their dainty fingers reaching to touch his pale chest, exposed between the open folds of his pale tunic.

"Always a pleasure to serve you, great Freyr." The blonde leans into him from one side, her shoulder rubbing his and her wide adoring eyes locking with his.

The redhead scoots around the opposite side and hooks her arm in his, leaning her head on his shoulder. Freyr spreads his arms, embracing both ladies in side hugs and stroking their upper arms, then he runs his fingers through the auburn hair, a satisfied smile plastered on his face.

"Okay, now, ladies. I need to show these lovely visitors where they will be residing and introduce them to their teacher." He gently nudges them forward and slaps them playfully on the backsides. "Now, run along."

Giggling, they run off, their flower-covered toes joyously covering the distance into the village.

The temptation to roll my eyes is too strong. "Are you serious?" I mutter, just loud enough for Elan and Naga to hear.

I know, right? Elan grumbles, her eyes fixed on the giggling elves disappearing.

Naga likes it. Naga thinks it sweet.

Distracted by one of the elves, Freyr leaves us to talk among ourselves.

Eir strokes around Naga's horns and runs a hand along the side of his face, and his eyes soften. "It is nice, Naga. A little strange that they're so obsessed with the god. But it's nice to see a realm that is full of peace and wishing the best for everyone." She fiddles with the lei hanging around her neck. Her expression is peaceful as she delicately touches the flowers, rolling their unusual shapes inside her fingers, studying their forms and intricate details. She observes the surroundings. "Such a beautiful realm. It may even be prettier than Midgard."

I lean my weight on one hip. "It's much nicer than it was in Muspelheim. I'm happy to admit to that." Fidgeting with the flowers on my lei, I frown. "But I don't know. It seems too over-the-top friendly and nice. It just doesn't sit right."

Eir hooks her elbow through mine and nudges me with her hip. "You're starting to sound like Hildr."

"Nice." I return her nudge. "I'm not that bad."

Eir smiles broadly. "Relax! Enjoy it and take it as it comes. If you're right and something sinister is hiding underneath all their friendliness, we'll deal with it then, just like we always do."

I push my lips into a smile. "You're right, Eir. Let's relax and enjoy this. It's not like we have anywhere else to go." The raw emotions at having been exiled from Asgard sour my smile with sadness.

Eir catches my tone. "We'll work it out. You won't be banished forever." She takes a long, deep breath of fresh air. "I just have a hunch. This land could be lucky for us, for you in particular."

I eye her with skepticism. "Lucky, you think. We'll see."

Something orange crawls on the ground in front of me, catching my attention. Ratatoskr stares up at me with beady eyes, arms crossed and foot tapping. He points his little claw at me. "There you are."

My jaw clenches in annoyance. *Right when I was hoping this realm would bring me some peace…* "What are you doing here?"

"Surt has a message for you." His nasal voice cuts through any remnants of peace left in my body.

"Oh, and what would that be?"

The rodent clears his voice and straightens his back, puffing out his chest. "Just because you managed to get your manipulative little butt out of Muspelheim doesn't mean that he can't find you. You owe him an answer, and he swears he will get it from you." Ratatoskr pauses, tilting his head to one side, and arches an eyebrow with amusement. "He will hunt you down through the realms and find you and get the answer from you. You may think you're safe from him and that he treated you harshly before, but you haven't seen what he can do. He's coming for you." The little rodent smiles cheekily, exposing his pointy teeth, his face awash with pleasure.

Chapter Two

Staring down at the little creature with black beady eyes, I'm suddenly overcome by a wave of deep, burning anger. Ratatoskr points a small claw at me, his other paw fisted on his hip, and my seething heightens. In Muspelheim, Elan and I went through a lot, and the little squirrel played a large part in that distress. I'm appalled by his aggression and yet another message disguised as an insult. Of course Surt, leader of the fire giants, is angry I was able to escape before he could force me to tell him Freya's location, but I'm not going to let him ruin my time on Alfheim by sending messages via this rude little red rodent. A creature like Ratatoskr, who takes pleasure in bringing agony to others by passing on insulting messages, is an abomination in this realm.

With fire in my belly, I tower over the little squirrel and shoo him away. "Run along, Ratatoskr. You've passed on the insult. So you can leave us be."

My stomach is soothed with satisfaction when shock covers his face.

"But… but what about the return message?" he stutters.

Shaking my head, a smile tugs at the edges of my mouth. "I'm not going to gratify that with a response. It's not worth my time. He's a large, lonely, and rather disturbed fire giant."

Ratatoskr's eyes sparkle, and his posture straightens. "Ah. There's an insult I can pass on."

"No. It's not a message or an insult. It's just fact."

The squirrel pauses and holds up a little paw. "But I'm still going to class it as an insult and a message."

Elan's golden scales brush against me, lightly nudging me aside as she stomps forward and roars right in Ratatoskr's face, baring her extensive array of teeth. Hot breath rushes over the furry little squirrel's face, pushing his fur backward.

The elves halt their everyday business, focusing on Elan, understanding filling their faces as they realize her showdown is with the red-furred squirrel.

Freyr approaches with a knowing smile. "Ah, Ratatoskr. I can see you have received a wonderfully appropriate welcome. You may leave now and take your offenses with you. This isn't the realm to bring insults. We are a peaceful community."

Ratatoskr waves a claw at the peaceful god. "You are wrong. I've brought many insults to this realm."

"You may have done so to the dark elves, but not to this side of the realm. It's prohibited to bring such negativity to the parts that I lead." Freyr waves a dismissive hand at him. "Now, run along like you've been told and leave us alone."

Ratatoskr turns to leave then peers over his shoulder and releases a disgusted snort at the god before scurrying toward Yggdrasil. Seeing the atrocious little rodent scurrying up the World Tree, I almost hug the sensual god, refraining at the last moment in case he takes it the wrong way. I smile, happy to see the back of that insulting little squirrel. Maybe I'll enjoy this realm after all.

Ratatoskr climbs a short way up the World Tree before calling over his shoulder, "You may think you're protected in this realm, Freyr, but you'd be surprised what lurks in its depths. Your peace and understanding"—he emphasizes the phrase in quotation marks with his claws—"has blinded you toward what's really going on."

Without waiting for a response, the red squirrel continues up Yggdrasil's trunk and disappears into the branches.

Freyr's body shakes with revulsion. "So much negativity in one tiny little package." After straightening his clothes, he glances back at the tree, and another shiver runs down his spine.

Despite my wariness of the good-looking blond god, I'm swamped by gratitude. "Thank you for getting rid of him. He made my life hell while I was stuck on Muspelheim. My situation was bad enough, yet he took so much pleasure in bringing me more discomfort and bad news when he could have supplied me with access to help." I run my hands down my black leather pants, my fingers finding the hole from my broken leg. When I pull my hands away, dirt covers my palms, and I'm embarrassed at my filthiness in front of these elves dressed in clean, pale colors.

Freyr smiles, and I can't fault his genuineness. "It's always my pleasure to get rid of any negativity that rodent brings." He extends a hand to me. "Come."

Without hesitating again, I oblige and clasp his hand, allowing myself to be led.

"See," Eir whispers. "He's not so bad. This place will be good." She loops her arm through mine.

I narrow my eyes slightly as I cast a side-glance at Eir, uncertainty still taunting me, but I allow more relaxation to seep in.

What are you doing, Kara? Apprehension laces Elan's voice.

"I'm going with the flow. But I'm still very hesitant," I whisper back.

Pursing her lips, she lets out an explosive breath that escapes in a whistle. *I'm glad. For a moment, I thought you let your guard down.*

I scrunch one side of my face. "I've been to a few realms now, and I've learned that isn't a good move."

Freyr slowly leads us through the light elves, who watch us, their faces filled with peace and caring that chills my stomach and stirs my anxiety. Everyone acting this way just doesn't seem natural. Nobody can be as peaceful and understanding as these elves.

Colorful foliage surrounds a small opening away from the flowing river. Eventually, the tropical plants muddle with trees of a different kind until the foliage changes, the leaves on the trees becoming smaller and rounder. Strange insects chirp in the leaves, and bird calls ring out in the distance as we weave through the sparsely spaced trunks.

Not much time passes before our travels take us to an area scattered with small cottages. Wooden boards mask the front surrounding the doors and the windows, framed on both sides by walls made of rocks. The side walls slope to the ground from the roof tip, covered with a neat mane of grass clipped an inch long and arching over the housetop. The cottages were built into a small hill, severed at the front and rear of the cottage.

"Aw. How quaint." Eir clasps her hands together, tilting her head to one side, studying the little buildings.

Freyr releases my grasp and draws his shoulders back. "This is our main village, Yantolos. It's the village where I spend most of my time. You should find the locals very accommodating here." He motions with a broad sweep of a hand toward the little cottages. "Unlike Asgard, the atmosphere is tranquil, and our village thrives on peace. If the surroundings, including the buildings, represent nature and harmony, it's easier to be peaceful on the inside." He rests his hand over his heart.

Eir, Naga thinks he speaks our language. Naga lowers his head to Eir's height, and she rubs under a scale on his cheek.

"I think you're right, Naga."

Oh, Vanir! Just look at those two. They're so love-struck with peace. Elan scoffs. Since neither Eir nor Naga responds, she clearly didn't reveal her thought to them.

Slowing my pace, I drop back to her leg and rub her scales, giving her a knowing look when she catches my eyes with hers. I completely understand where she's coming from. Everything seems too good to be true. Attempting to be open-minded, I add, "They are quaint, Eir. After Muspelheim, it's a pleasant change."

We follow Freyr through the village to where the cottages thin and several more trees provide shelter. Stopping in front of a cabin with a stained natural timber facade, he spreads his arms wide. "This is your home while you're here. It's part of the outskirts of our village, Yantolos."

He twists the door handle and pushes it open, letting it swing wide to expose a cozy interior. Floral designs and trees are engraved into the edges of the wooden furniture.

Elan lowers an eye to the opening, where her lips would barely fit through. *Where can we sleep? I'm having trouble fitting my head through the door.*

Smiling at her attempt at humor, I tap her front leg. "Come on, Elan. Out of the way. You and Naga, with your big tough hides, can sleep outside."

Elan huffs, and a coat of hot air washes over me. *We've always gotta sleep outside.* Casting a side glance at me, she lands the confused Freyr with a cheeky smile showing off her ferocious rows of teeth. *It's all good. I don't like sleeping indoors anyway.*

Squeezing past Elan, I walk inside, my boots clunking on the wooden floor.

Floorboards squeak as Eir follows, her mouth

agape. "Wow! I could live here. This is so much nicer than our apartment. It makes our accommodation on Asgard look more like the dormitories at the academy."

On the far side of the room, a fire burns in a fireplace embedded in the stone wall. The outside temperature seems cooler, but after Muspelheim's heat, everything seems cool. A long stone bench serves as a bottom lip to the gaping hole, and a stack of wood cut to a good burning size lies neatly underneath the bench. Stone tiles form a broad platform near the bench, leading down to a wooden floor a couple of feet into the room. Two single beds line the sides of the stone bench at a safe distance from the burning hole under stained wooden beams that line the ceiling, pointing up in the middle. A small, stained wooden duchess table stands on one side of the room with a stool sitting in front. On the other is a cupboard sided with a chest of drawers. Even though the cottage is humble, like Eir said, it seems nicer than our accommodations on Asgard.

Freyr's voice interrupts my thoughts. "I hope you like it."

"It is lovely. I adore it." Eir clasps her hands in front of her, her eyes wide as they complete another circuit of the small interior. She smiles. "I wish my place in Asgard was like this."

Freyr smiles broadly. "Then perhaps this could be a second home." He throws his hands wide and bows slightly. "Make yourself comfortable and relax. We'll have to go and find your magic instructor. I think you should be introduced straightaway—that is, as soon as you're settled."

I slide my quiver off my shoulders, removing it from my back with the sword attached, relieved after having worn it for so long. Even though I'm apprehensive about the elves being actually as peaceful as they're portraying, I don't sense any physical threat. I sigh when cold air brushes over the sweaty spot left by the weapons on my back. At the same time, that reminds me of how dirty I am underneath my damaged uniform.

As though reading my mind, Freyr adds, "On second thought, maybe you would like to freshen up and find new clothes before you meet your trainer."

My jaw drops at the thought. I've been wearing my Valkyrie fighting leathers for as long as I remember. It would be strange, almost discomfiting, to change into whatever clothes the elves supplied. However, I have to admit washing myself and ridding my body of the dirt and grime of Muspelheim would be a welcome relief. I can feel dried sweat caked in dirt lining my uniform, and my lips curl in disgust. Ignoring the discomfort and exhaustion riddling my body, I eye the two beds with enthusiasm, wondering which is mine.

I place my weapons against the cupboard, the arrows rattling in the quiver and the sword hilt clunking against the wall. My gaze again falls on the bed, which is calling to my exhausted body.

My thoughts are pulled back into reality when a loud voice fills the room, and I cringe at the volume and the disruption of my peace.

"So. Who are my victims?"

A plump elf fills the doorway. His belly protrudes over the thin belt secured around the waist of his tunic. His spiky blond hair stands on end a couple of inches long, and pale stubble covers his chin. The messy appearance seems odd, compared to the elves I met previously. Many elves seemed to prefer hair down to the shoulders, if not longer. His round cheeks spread with a smile as his eyes ignite with excitement, and his jolly demeanor counteracts the threat of us being his victims.

"Aymar! You're here early." Freyr clasps the chubby elf's upper arm in a friendly greeting. "I was just suggesting that the Valkyries may want to clean up and rest a little before starting their lessons." The god peers at me from under a raised eyebrow. "Especially Kara."

The elf enters a foot inside the cottage and bows with a slight dip to the blond god. "Forgive me, great

Freyr. I'm keen to meet my new students. I missed the gathering for their welcome into the realm, and I wanted to meet them in person. I've just arrived back from visiting another village. They needed some of my magic expertise." He chuckles and places a hand over his heart, briefly lowering his eyes to the ground. "I'm afraid my reputation precedes me."

"You do have an impressive talent." Freyr leads him farther into the room with a hand on the elf's back. "Let me introduce you. This is Eir and Kara."

"And your reputation precedes you, young Kara." He bows his head at me. "And, of course, your peaceful friend Eir as well. I'm sure you'll feel right at home here," he tells Eir.

Surprise flashes over Freyr's face. "I didn't realize you're so familiar with these young wingless Valkyries."

Aymar chuckles, and his belly jiggles. "It's unusual, I know." A slight flush covers his cheeks. "Forgive me. I'm not a stalker, I promise. I just take an interest in new magic users." He searches the room and frowns. "Where are your two friends?"

"Naga and Elan are outside. They're too big to fit in here." Eir motions toward the outside.

A frown of confusion creases the elf's face. "I mean your wingless Valkyrie friends with magic."

"Thor thought it best for Kara's learning if there

were fewer of them to teach," Freyr explains. "That way, there will be more one-on-one training. He asked Eir to join her so she wasn't the only Valkyrie and because Eir is the peaceful one of the four of them."

Aymar shoves his sleeves halfway up his arms, exposing their thickness, and faces Eir. "Interesting choice and a strangely wise one from the god of thunder." A broad smile spreads across his face. "It's nice to know he's learning to use his brain." When he spots the confusion on Freyr's face, he laughs and waves dismissively. "Aah, I'm joking! I thought you knew me better than that." Turning to me, he asks, "Is that your big dragon out there?"

Still on edge after Muspelheim, I ask, "Aren't there two dragons out there?"

Aymar nods. "Indeed. I mean the big golden one."

"Yes, that's my dragon."

"Ooh. Impressive." Turning to Eir, he clasps her hand. "And yours must be the blue one."

Eir's eyes light up with pride. "Yes. Naga. His name is Naga."

He clicks his tongue against the top of his mouth. "Such an adorable breed."

"Yes. He is." Her voice is enthusiastic, yet her brows knit together as she casts me a strange look, which reads as though the elf is sweet but a little odd.

I nod in agreement.

Aymar releases Eir's hand and scans the cottage briefly before his eyes land on a bowl displaying all sorts of tropical fruits and nuts I've never seen before. "Food!" He dashes to the table and clasps a palm-sized firm red fruit in his meaty hand. Turning to me, he asks, "Do you mind?"

From his size, that seemed a strange food for him to consume. He turns toward Freya, then Eir, then me.

I'm about to shake my head despite longing to taste the unique display in front of me. The thought of eating some of those exotic fruits makes my mouth water. I would love to have them in Asgard, if I ever get to return.

I almost breathe a sigh of relief when Freyr interrupts. "No. They're not for you. They're for our guests. You should know that. There's plenty of food for you in the food hall."

The large elf cackles and rubs his stomach. "Of course, of course. I just can't help it. I'm always hungry." He releases the fruit into the bowl with a soft thud. "So, should we get started?"

Exhaustion overcomes me at the thought, and his vibrant energy and joyous attitude drain me. The fatigue seems embedded deep within my body, settled into the marrow of my bones. As keen as I am to learn magic, I'm tired and could use some rest. Unconsciously, my shoulders sag.

Relief seeps into my body when Freyr answers, "Don't be ridiculous. Can't you see Kara is exhausted? She's been through such an ordeal. Her magic training is important, but she will learn more tomorrow after a good night's rest. Both Kara and Eir will clean up and relax and recharge for the afternoon and practice under your guidance tomorrow. After all, this is a realm of peace and relaxation. Our magic stems from joy and happiness, not from anxiety and stress."

Aymar clutches his hands together respectfully. "Of course, you're correct. Right, then. I'll come and collect you both first thing in the morning." He shuffles out the door, his long white tunic flowing around his thighs, his love handles wobbling.

I'm happy to see his enthusiastic face disappear, letting me relax. At the moment, his cheerful and encouraging attitude is exhausting. My relief turns to admiration as I face Freyr. "Thank you. I do need rest. Where can we wash up?" I brush a hand over my leather uniform and cringe at the crusted dirt. "And this uniform could certainly use a wash or replacement."

His broad smile is cheeky. "We all wash in the lake not far from here."

My jaw drops. "What? In the open?"

The smile widens. "Yes. I guess you could say that. Nobody here is worried about a little exposed skin. In this realm, it's not frowned upon. We're all comfortable with our bodies."

"Oh, how nice." Disapproval seeps into my voice. Looking down at my filthy clothes, I can feel the grime crawling on my skin. I return my gaze to his cheeky eyes. "I'm not uncomfortable in my skin, but I still prefer to bathe in private."

"That may be so, but it's the only place."

I long to wipe the smile off his face. It doesn't matter if he's a god. Placing my hands on my hips, I ask, "Can't you conjure up some kind of bathtub in our little quarters so Eir and I can bathe in private?"

"Sorry. The river is the only place available," he says without regret.

- Chapter Four -

I swallow, not sure how to take the god's lack of concern for our privacy. My eyes narrow as my brow pushes down into a frown.

Freyr interrupts my scrutiny. "You'll find the way to the lake just outside." He points to his right, toward a wall. "The path leads through the forest to the outside of the village. It's not too far." He turns as if to leave. "I'll check later to see how your stay is going. In the meantime, help yourself to the food in this bowl until the next mealtime." He nods briefly toward the bowl of fruit and nuts he rescued from Aymar's stomach before the door clicks shut behind him.

Eir's and my gazes meet.

You better have a bath, Kara. Elan's voice pierces our thoughts. *I can smell you from here.*

A smile lights Eir's face momentarily and widens

until her laughter rings throughout the room. "You dragons never cease to amaze me." She slaps a thigh lightly. "Actually, I think our lives would be boring without you."

I glare at Eir. "I don't know about boring, but the dragons certainly add some fun." I call back to Elan, "I still don't like the idea of bathing in the open."

Oh, Kara. Relax. Naga and I will stand guard, Elan says.

The dirt clinging to my hair pulls when I rub my arm, reminding me just how filthy I am. "All right. I would love to freshen up. First, though, we need to find some clean clothes."

At the end of my bed, the chest of drawers not far from where I dropped my quiver catches my eye.

As though reading my thoughts, Eir approaches it. "Perhaps there's something in here." She yanks open the top drawer to dip in a hand and extract several small lacy undergarments. "I hope these aren't our clothes." A sly smirk spreads across her face.

After tossing the underwear back into the drawer and closing it, she opens the next. "These look a little more appropriate." Pressed between her hands is a folded pale-blue garment. Holding it at the shoulders, she lets the fabric hang to the ground, lining it against herself. "I could match Naga." Dreamily, she smiles as her gaze trails down the dress, dropping to her boots. She cringes. "I don't think the boots go with it." She drapes it over the bed and retrieves from the drawer a pile of folded garments of different pale colors, including powder blue, pink, green, and lilac.

My eyes widen at the fabrics foreign to my body. All the garments available are dainty and feminine, constructed of soft, flowing cotton. At the bottom of the pile of dim colors, pale lemon catches my eye. The color sparks a vision of the dress complementing Elan's golden scales, and I reach and pull it from Eir's grasp. I hold it close, just far enough that it won't rub against my filthy fighting uniform and skin. The dress flows to the ground, billowing out from the waist, which appears slightly bigger than my size, a belt draping from the material hooks. "I guess this will do." I eye the fabric apprehensively. "It's going to be weird not wearing my fighting leathers. I've worn Valkyrie fighting leathers almost since the day I joined the academy."

An understanding look covers Eir's face. "Clearly, we're not here to fight physically. Magic shouldn't necessitate the extended physical movements that require our fighting leathers."

A heaviness fills my heart as I gaze longingly at my quiver and flying sword. "Our weapons are probably null and void here."

After placing the remaining folded garments back into the drawer, Eir pulls open the third drawer, revealing various sandals. A small squeal fills the room. "These are so pretty." Rummaging through the varieties, she pulls out a matching pair of sandals and holds them against the dress she placed over the bed. Powder-blue flowers line the strap curving over the arch of the foot. Pride fills her face as she places them on the floor in front of the dress. "I, for one, won't be carrying weapons." Her mouth twists to one side. "I don't even think I'll miss them. I can't wait to practice the magic we will learn here." She rummages through the drawer again and pulls out a matching pair of sandals with lemon-colored flowers. Holding them up excitedly, she swivels around to show me before comparing them to the gown I chose. She quirks an eyebrow as though daring me to disagree with the match.

I take them from her and snatch up my dress.

Eir grabs a handful of undergarments for both of us. "Come on. Let's go. I haven't even been to Muspelheim, nor have I been fighting, yet I still feel grotty." She holds up a couple of undergarments, assessing them, and a smirk grows on her face. "It's almost as though they knew what size we were before we came."

I shrug. "I can't imagine guessing our size would be that hard. I haven't seen an overweight Valkyrie yet. We're all toned and conditioned for fighting unless we're pregnant, and that's extremely rare."

After closing the door behind ourselves, we head down the path weaving its way through the forest.

With her face tilted to the sky, Eir studies the tree-tops and foliage surrounding the path. "I can't believe how pretty it is here. Smell that fresh air." She inhales noisily through her nose. "It makes me not miss the hard stone walls and marble buildings of Asgard."

My feet falter. "Do you mean that you would leave Asgard for here?"

Eir purrs, her voice filled with richness and warmth. "I'm not planning on leaving Asgard, but this would definitely make a nice holiday home."

Birds chirp, their calls filling the silence of the forest, reminding me of Midgard and relaxing my muscles. "I can see what you mean. It is pretty, but I still miss my home."

Peering at me over her shoulder, Eir says, "You probably miss it more because you've been banished."

I scan the forest, studying the different formations

of the ground pushing up into hills, and I take in the surrounding array of trees forming the forest. "Possibly."

The path thins and cuts through tall reeds that thicken as we progress. The crumpling of foliage under the dragons' talons changes from snapping dried leaves and twigs to moister sounds as the reeds open onto a lake.

Before me, the beauty of the scenery briefly pushes aside the uncomfortable thought of bathing in the open. Tall trees line the edges of the lake, backing away into thick forests.

"This must be it," I say.

"It is beautiful." Eir sounds breathless.

Elan nods at me. *We have your back. As promised, Naga and I will watch out for visitors.*

I strip away my filthy, tattered Valkyrie fighting uniform, a potent smell of sweat and dirt wafting up to assault my nose. My lip curls. I definitely need to clean up. My fingers brush over the hole in the thigh of my pants, reminding me of the broken bone that was sticking out of the fabric not so long before. The terror of what happened in Muspelheim flashes to the forefront of my mind, making me want to wash away the reminder. I toss the tattered black leather uniform to the edge of the reeds, glad to be rid of the horrible smell and thickly caked-on dirt from that hot realm filled with lava rivers and arid stone.

A cool breeze brushes my skin, and goose bumps prickle my flesh. Something swoops down, gliding overhead with large wings stretching wide. Instantly, I cover my body with my hands to guard against prying eyes before snapping out of it and taking a more defensive stance. My heart races as I take in the multiple colors of the creature's body and feathered wings. Its shape reminds me of an oversized bird.

The creature doesn't stop, and I decide to head into the water. Anything could fly above or peer through the reeds. The tepid water engulfs my skin, soaking into my underwear and restoring my flesh with instant freshness. I can almost feel the dirt washing away and the water cleansing my pores.

When the water reaches my shoulders, I can no longer refuse the call of relaxation. Pushing backward, I float on my back, stroking my hands beside my body, taking in the clean blue sky, and letting the water work its magic on my sore muscles.

Something disturbs the water, causing it to splash around the edges of my face, and I sit up, looking for the cause, only to find Eir following my example.

"It looks like it's just what you needed."

"It is quite relaxing." I lay back again, letting the

water frame my face. My arms tread water softly by my side. After a while, relaxation causes my eyes to drift closed, and prying them open takes an effort. I force myself upright and set to work washing the dirt and grime from my hair and body, gladly removing all traces of Muspelheim.

More colorful winged creatures fly overhead, their large beaks pointing forward and their long legs dragging behind. Their vicious build is betrayed by every color of the rainbow.

Movement on the shore pulls my attention to the dragons, whose eyes are trained on the creatures yet still searching the forest, on guard for any other disturbances to our bathing time. I smile. Our trusty companions are always watching out for us, which quashes my initial worry over being watched.

The flying creatures disappear, and my eyes droop as the excitement passes. I call to Eir, "I have to go. I'm so tired I could fall asleep in this water. It's relaxed every muscle in my body."

A screech fills the air, and tension springs back into my muscles. I stand in the water, my eyes alert as I search every part of the blue sky for something ferocious. Coming up empty, I train my eyes on Elan. Every muscle in her body is flexing as she cranes her neck to the sky. After another fruitless search, my eyes connect with Eir's, my confusion mirrored on her face.

"Perhaps it's nothing seri—"

Her words are cut short by another screech. Our eyes widen, and the hairs on my neck stand on end as I catch sight of the creature.

Chapter Five

*D*ragon scales! *Elan cries.* It looks just like the *zmey but the wrong color.*

I drop into the water, stopping at chin level, gazing into the sky. The liquid suddenly seems cold, the chill creeping into my spine. "Loki can't be here, can he?" My lips are numb, and I struggle to get the words out.

You know it's a different color, right?

I squint at Elan, annoyed that she's pointing out the obvious. "I can see that. Thanks."

Eir places a hand on my shoulder, warming my bare skin. "I doubt it's Loki. There's more than one zmey. Loki has to fashion his shape off something."

The thought of a zmey and Loki brings my attention to the scar on my shoulder from where Loki's zmey marked me. A book from the academy library had mentioned the zmey and how their mark inserts magic into the receiver.

As though reading my thoughts, Eir whispers, "I know Loki can shapeshift into different forms with different colors, but I doubt this is him."

Suspicious, I gaze back at the creature passing overhead. "I hope you're right. I keep feeling like something is lurking in the peacefulness of this realm, waiting to surprise us with danger."

An understanding smile passes over Eir's face. "That's just post-traumatic stress." She rubs my back. "You've been through a lot, and you went through more when you went to Muspelheim. Not only that, you were pretty much alone. Only Thor knew where you were, and he was unconscious."

My teeth gritted together. "Ratatoskr knew where I was. But that terrible little rodent wouldn't do anything to help."

Eir nods. "And that's a lot to deal with." Her warm fingers briefly massage my neck as we watch the zmey disappear into the distance. "Come on. Let's get dressed so you can catch up on some rest." Deep, dark circles under her eyes emphasize her exhaustion, an unusual look for a Valkyrie.

Water drips from our skin back into the lake as we trudge toward dry ground. After toweling off, we dress in our fresh undergarments, followed by our pale gowns. The fabric is strange against my skin, flowing loosely, almost inserting insecurity into me.

Compared to the leather, the fabric is light and soft and doesn't cling to me.

Eir chuckles. "You look feminine and beautiful. You should wear garments like this more often."

Her pale-blue gown drapes to the ground, swaying slightly around her ankles. A thin belt straps the waist closer to her skin. It brings out all her attractive features, accentuated by her pale-brown hair falling loosely around her face. She looks almost as pretty as the winged Valkyries. Actually… she looks *better* than the perfect blond battle maidens. The wingless Valkyries have often been viewed as less appealing than our winged counterparts, except the wingless have more variety in our looks and more originality. To others who don't strictly favor the winged Valkyries, this seems more attractive.

Placing a hand on her upper arm, I'm stunned momentarily by the caress of the material around my thighs and legs. I focus on Eir and say sincerely, "So do you. You look gorgeous. Not that you don't normally." I touch the fabric of her skirt and rub it between my fingers and thumb. "This color brings out your beautiful eyes and complements your skin." I squint. "Somehow, it highlights your peaceful and understanding nature."

Stooping, we gather our old fighting leathers. I hold mine away from my beautiful lemon gown, determined to keep off the dirt, blood, and sweat. I don't need any ugly marks on it before I return to the village.

A puff of breeze drags the scent of the uniform upward, and I screw up my nose. "Wow! I certainly needed a wash. Now that I'm clean, I can smell just how bad it was." With one hand, I hold the uniform up, twisting it to have a closer look at it. "It's almost ready to be thrown out, I think. I'm going to miss it."

"Don't you carry a spare in your saddlebag?" Eir asks.

My eyes widen in surprise. "I do. I'd completely forgotten. I've never had to use it before because I've always gone back to Asgard, where I've got a wardrobe full of them."

The dresses sway around our hips and legs as we make our way back to the cabin. The feeling is strange yet refreshing at the same time when a cool breeze sneaks its way up my skirt.

The lake's glimmering water catches my eye through the reeds when I peer over my shoulder at the lagging dragons. "Do you think Freyr was teasing us over this being a public bathing spot?"

A broad smile spreads across Eir's face. "I wouldn't be surprised. Although they probably do have a bathing area, I don't think it would be as bad as he's making out."

After the ordeal I've been through, the thought of being provoked, even in a friendly manner, makes my muscles weak. "Why would he do that?"

Eir shrugs. "Probably because he senses that you're not like the elves, who are free with their love giving. I'm sure he's harmless, or else Freya and Thor wouldn't have left you in his care."

We weave our way through the trees, eventually catching sight of the cottage. Exhaustion overwhelms me. "I think I could sleep for a week."

"You go ahead and sleep." Eir hands me her small bag of dirty clothes. "I'm going to meet some of the locals."

Wearily, I nod and head to the cottage and pry open the door without even looking over my shoulder to see if the dragons are following. I toss Eir's dirty laundry on the floor at the end of her bed and my destroyed fighting leathers in a small waste bin in the corner, happy to be rid of the smell. The bowl of fruit and nuts on the table catches my eye, and my stomach warbles as I grab a piece of strange fruit out of the bowl. I know I should sit at the table to eat, but my tiredness and hunger match each other. I take a bite, the soft, juicy flesh squishing in my mouth as I climb onto my bed. The sweetness spreads over my taste buds, bringing a groan from my throat, and I lower onto my side as I chew. It tastes delicious, reminding me of a mango from Midgard, yet slightly different.

Even with the added excitement of the fruit's juices, my eyes drift shut, unable to combat my exhaustion any longer. My hand holding the fruit drops to the bed, and I swallow, my growling stomach ignored as I fall into a deep sleep.

Strange dreams and nightmarish memories flood back into my thoughts, images of Muspelheim, Surt, and the dragon emerging from the lava river. Ratatoskr sits on a rocky ledge inside the cave walls entrapping me, pointing his claw in my direction and holding his stomach, laughing. I toss and turn, my sleep restless.

A loud bang startles me out of my nightmare, and I sit upright, eyes wide as I gaze at a figure in a soft dress, standing in the doorway. I blink, trying to clear away the remnants of the nightmare and focusing on the new arrival.

"I'm so sorry. Did I wake you?" Eir runs a hand down the pale-blue fabric cascading down her body.

Realizing that no threat is present, I wipe the sleep from my eyes and yawn. "Yeah." I stretch my arms to the ceiling, surprised to find that my arms are covered in the juice of the fruit I was eating. Spotting it on the floor, I realize I must have knocked it during my sleep.

"You've been asleep for hours. Clearly, you needed it, but it's time for some food." Her eyes drop to the squashed piece of fruit lying on my bedcovers.

I spot the juice stain on the light fabric. Uselessly, I wipe at the mess then give up, stretching my arms out to the sides.

"Perhaps you need something more filling than fruit."

The thought of food causes my stomach to groan, and I throw my legs over the side of the bed.

"You're right. I need something more substantial too." After peeling the sticky fruit off the floor, I throw it into the trash with my old uniform. "I can't remember the last time I ate a decent meal." I touch my face and find a gooey residue around my mouth.

Eir smiles. "I see you did try to eat something. I guess it didn't go so well?"

I shake my head. "I was so tired I couldn't even eat more than a mouthful."

Eir dips a white hand towel into a bowl of water resting on a bench near the door and hands it to me. I wipe the residue from my face then work on the bed cover, pulling the cloth away with a satisfied grin when the messy patch disappears.

I place the towel back into the bowl. "Now, I'm famished." I swirl the cloth in the water a few times, leaving a slight taint in the water.

"Come." Eir indicates for me to follow.

Resting the towel in the water, I slip on my flowered sandals and close the door behind myself, matching Eir's pace toward the village.

We pass a few cottages before curiosity gets the better of me. "Where are we going?"

"They have a communal hall where they eat together."

We reach a sizeable open-air area sheltered by long vines strung from one side to the other. Tables laden with an extensive array of food stretch in rows with bench seats lining their sides. Not a cooking fire or kitchen is in sight. Delicious smells waft to my nose, and my mouth waters, almost tasting the different meats and vegetables as I eye the flavorsome display on the large serving trays. It reminds me of Odin's food hall, except this impressive display is for the common light elves of Alfheim. Large lilac flowers drape from the vined canopy overhead, and their scent mixes with the smells of the delicious food.

The sight was endearing and utterly different from Asgard and the stone rooms held together with marble pillars.

"How strange." I run my fingers over a low-hanging vine. "It reminds me of the academy mess hall except it's much nicer." I inhale deeply. "And the food is much better."

Several elves progress into the canopied area and sit on a couple of tables not far from us. Eir steps over the bench seat, threading her legs under the food-loaded table, and I sit next to her.

"Yes. I had lunch here when you were sleeping. That was divine." Eir picks at a small morsel at the corner of a serving plate and places it in her mouth, groaning. "This looks and tastes even better."

Chapter Six

Eir wasn't exaggerating. The food here is delicious. The choice is almost overwhelming, and when I sample the individual dishes, I nearly melt onto my seat from the flavors. After one mouthful, I know I'll have to keep up some physical training or risk growing to the size of our magic instructor, Aymar.

Grabbing the serving spoon, I cleave off small portions of several dishes and load them onto my plate. Suddenly, my arm is nudged from the side as someone climbs onto the bench beside me, knocking the last portion off the serving spoon and onto the table. A frown creases my forehead as I eye the wasted food, my arm still poised. Obliviously, this person reaches a plump arm over the top of mine, shoving it aside to grasp another spoon and serve several spoonfuls onto their plate.

A little taken aback by the sudden appearance and roughness of this person, I face the owner of the arm to find our new magic instructor. Unaware of my annoyance, Aymar continues to dish up everything he can reach, plopping it onto his plate until the contents overflow onto the wooden table. In only a few seconds, the plump instructor forks the contents into his mouth.

Repressed frustration and anger from my trip to Muspelheim bubble to the surface. Instead of letting it out on Aymar, I cap the steaming pot and take a moment to study the group. I'm not sure an antipeaceful display will go over well among these peaceful elves. Taking in each movement, my mind whirs as it processes the information. The loud smacking of lips cuts through my thoughts, accompanied by a peal of boisterous laughter muffled by food. Aymar's head is thrown back, his mouth full and open as he laughs over something the elf on his other side has mentioned. Attempting to ignore him, I find it hard not to scowl as I continue loading food onto my plate. By the time I have enough choices, Aymar's mannerisms have crept under my skin.

My eyes connect with Eir's, and she smiles knowingly. Her familiar peacefulness helps push aside my annoyance, giving me the strength to remain pleasant. I could be in this new realm for quite some time, and I need to learn to accept these elves' customs and how they interact. I return Eir's smile and fork some food into my mouth, groaning. The flavors melt over my tongue, filling my mouth with the perfect combination of savory and sweet, instantly improving my mood. The food is unlike anything I've tasted before. The flavors put me in a light trance, putting everything into a better light and even temporarily blocking out Aymar's lack of table manners.

Slowly, I scan the open hall, taking in the scenery and its construction. Long vines climb up posts that hold up an open frame acting as a roof, strung together with long, thin beams. Vines are twisted around the wood and draped from one shaft to the other, blocking out the night sky, and lilac flowers mixed with fairy lights droop between the emerald-green leaves. A light fragrance wafts through the air, a sweetness similar to honeysuckle. The tension in my shoulders slowly leaks away when I inhale deeply, replaced by tendrils of serenity until Aymar faces me, the slapping of his lips growing louder beside me. The muscles in my neck tighten as I clench my jaw, working hard to muster a diplomatic face before I look at him.

My smile is a thin line. "You have some appetite."

He chuckles again, displaying a mouth full of

mushed food, his arms resting on both sides of his plate. He forks a baked potato onto his plate, ready to dig in, but he pauses. "You could say that." He chuckles some more. "Let's just say the food is so delicious here that I can't get enough." He rubs his belly extravagantly. "As you can see."

In addition to his obsession with food, something else strikes me as odd when Eir says, "It's quite strange to have a teacher sit next to us." She studies him over the top of me, managing to say this in her uncritical way. Not a line on her face shows the harshness I would've expressed. At the thought, envy wraps its tentacles around my heart. Eir can be so direct yet diplomatic at the same time.

Aymar leans back, his belly jiggling with a chuckle. "Of course I'm sitting with you. It's not a *school*. Or an academy, in your case." His eyebrow rises as he swallows his mouthful, his gaze gliding between Eir and me. "Although I hear you finished the academy a couple of years back."

"Yes, we did." I push some food around on my plate, deciding which delicious morsel to try next. "I guess Eir is saying that it's usual for someone of importance to sit at the same table as us during a group gathering. Usually, they sit at a different table." Scanning the open hall, I realize no such tables exist. Even Freyr is sitting with the elves of the village, albeit among many pretty female elves.

Aymar forks some more food into his mouth, a broad, knowing smile plastered on his face. "Not in Alfheim. The elves treat each other as equals." He waves a hand broadly, indicating the group. "We can all do magic. I'm just a better teacher." He shrugs. "Maybe my magic is better than some of the others." He acts as though that's not a big deal. "You should get used to it. If you like me enough, I'll probably sit next to you all the time."

Not sure how to respond, I shovel some of the food into my mouth. Once again, the flavors melt over my taste buds, and a small groan escapes my throat as I chew. This food seems to fiddle with the brain's receptors, instantly placing me in a better mood. Despite Aymar's eating habits, I believe I could grow to like him. He seems jolly and friendly, which makes it hard to think of any reason I wouldn't enjoy his company.

The dry scratching of my eyelids reminds me of my exhaustion, and I put down some of my crankiness over his eating habits to my extreme tiredness. The nap before dinner didn't take away the ordeal or the exhaustion of Muspelheim. As I scoop up another forkful of food, thoughts of Elan and Naga enter my head, and I turn to our teacher. "Are the dragons getting fed? Or do they have to go hunting?"

His eyes widen, and all humor drops from his face. "Oh, no. The dragons have been fed." He stops eating for a moment, stirring uneasiness in me. "We don't want them to go hunting. There are rare creatures on Alfheim we don't want killed. The only way to stop this is to feed them before they become hungry."

I don't have to fake my smile. "That's great. It's nice to know the dragons are also looked after."

He spreads his arms wide, palms up, almost hitting me and the elf on his other side. "When you have magic like the light elves', you can just produce the food in an instant. It's easy. Why wouldn't we feed the dragons?"

My mouth stretches into a thin line. That all seems too easy. As though to emphasize a point, the food on the table before us vanishes, replaced by an array of desserts. With wide eyes, I push my plate aside and gather a few sweet foods into a bowl. Shoveling my spoon into a red jellylike substance, I raise it to my mouth. It wobbles ungracefully on my spoon and evaporates on my tongue, smothering it in sweetness as it instantly turns liquid. The next item is creamy and frozen into a semisolid, melting instantly when the slightly heated spoon slices through it.

Chunks of a fruit's soft orange flesh blends through the light frozen cream, and the two combined melt on my tongue.

Aymar devours the dessert with even fewer manners than his main meal. I push the displeasing sight aside, finding my memory of the lake jerked to the surface by the bright colors. "When we were at the lake today, we saw a strange creature. It looks like a zmey, only it's a different color."

"Yes. That's still a zmey. We have them here. They are revered."

My jaw drops for a moment as I try to overcome my shock, contradicting memories flooding through my head. "Really? They're not Loki, are they?" The words stagger out against my will, and I know I probably sound ridiculous.

He chuckles again, tugging at the point of an ear before scratching his stubbly chin. "My dear, zmeys are revered because of their magic and because they mark people, giving them more magic. That magic grows stronger than an ordinary elf's magic alone. I don't know how you think that this would make them Loki." He holds up a thick finger. "Although I hear that the zmey on Asgard was Loki, and that is how you two developed magic." His curious eyes land on both of us.

I hold my breath then mutter, "Yes. For some

reason, Loki decided to mark me. Then later, he marked my three wingless Valkyrie friends. We still haven't worked out the reason yet. Is it normal for a zmey to randomly pick people?"

Amusement dances in his eyes. "Magical beings are mysterious creatures. And a zmey with the gift to give magic to their victims is even more mysterious."

Using the tip of my spoon, I push the dessert around on my bowl, frowning despite the delicious taste. I study Eir from the corner of my eye, realizing she also seems to be having trouble deciphering the cryptic information, and her eyes remain thoughtful as she spoons more food into her mouth.

Aymar loads more food onto his plate, and my eyes widen as some of the contents slop over the sides onto the table. I'm amazed at how much he can eat. He's almost as bad as Thor, except, based on his shape, I'm sure Aymar doesn't get as much exercise from training on the sparring field to burn it off.

The trainer's voice cuts through our silence. "Apparently, I've got to give you until tomorrow before we can start training." His face reflects the disappointment in his voice. "Freyr insists that you need some more rest. I guess he's right."

I jump as his hand touches my bare arm underneath the loose, flowing sleeve of my pale-lemon gown, sending a strange jolt up the limb. The unex-pected touch brings back some of the tension of Muspelheim.

His eyes flick over me, noticing my visible reaction. "Don't fret. I'm just injecting you with some rejuvenating power. It won't disturb your sleep. In fact, combined with a good night's sleep, it will help you recoup quicker."

"Oh." I lay my hand briefly over my thumping heart, feeling breathless. "Thank you."

"My pleasure." After removing his hand, he reaches across the table and touches Eir's hand, who also jolts.

A knowing smile creeps across his face. "I can't leave you out. Just in case you're feeling tired."

Eir retracts her hand and studies it for any markings. When she doesn't find any, she smiles at him. "Thank you."

The large trainer smiles broadly. "Now, remember this isn't Asgard. You don't need your fighting leathers." He screws up his nose in distaste. "What you're wearing is perfectly acceptable."

Feeling overwhelmed, I push back from the table. "I'm finished. I can't eat anymore, and I want to get an early night."

Eir mirrors my actions. "Me too." She turns to Aymar. "I guess we'll see you in the morning."

"Bright and early. Breakfast is at sunrise. If you're

not at the training ground afterward, I'll be coming to get you." His singsong voice follows us out of the hall.

Chapter Seven

Two massive thumping sounds cut through my dreams, startling me awake. When I turn to the window with wide eyes, searching for the source, Elan's excited face greets me. She exposes her extensive array of vicious teeth in what I now know is her smile, even if it does look more threatening than friendly.

Did someone mention breakfast? Because if they did, they are instantly my new best friend. Her golden eyes flash with disappointment when she realizes our cabin lacks the kind of food she is after. After shifting to a sitting position, I push off my bed, the long cotton nightie flowing to my knees. As I'm about to break the bad news to her that we don't have any food to give them, a couple of thuds catch her attention. Naga and Elan face the other way, and I clasp the ledge of the window. Two large carcasses are now lying on the dried leaves and twigs.

Without waiting for approval, Elan and Naga tear at the uncooked flesh, several bits devoured before I can take a good look.

Unfastening the latch, I pry the window open. "Where did you get them from?"

Elan shrugs, her golden-yellow wings splaying momentarily. *No idea. I guess the elves know we're hungry after our long flight.*

They both tear off some of the flesh and swallow it.

"Where did you go?"

We just flew wherever our hearts took us.

Naga lifts his head long enough to fix his large blue eyes on me. *It's gorgeous out there. Naga is in love with this land. There are many clear blue lakes surrounded by tropical forests that spread almost from one end of the realm to the other.*

Elan jolts her neck as she swallows a large piece of flesh whole, her golden eyes bright either from her appreciation of the beauty of this realm or from the taste of the animal flesh. *Let me tell you, it's a much nicer place than Muspelheim.*

"You don't need to tell me. I can see that from here." My gaze travels past the feasting dragons to the trees beyond, taking in the beauty and peaceful-ness of the forest. "Although, did you say the whole realm is covered in a forest like this?"

Yes, the whole realm, Elan says. *It's covered with waterfalls, lakes, rivers, and beautiful greenery. There are some mountains made of stone. It looks similar to parts of Midgard, if not better.*

The sound of tearing flesh continues, and I screw up my nose as I watch her devour another piece. "I'll leave you to it."

Elan shrugs, swallows the portion in her mouth, then clasps what remains of the animal carcass between her front talons, securing it in place as she tears off another chunk. I let the curtains fall shut and spot Eir still asleep on her bed. I thought she looked peaceful awake, and it always surprises me how she looks more peaceful while asleep. Her light-brown locks fan out on the pillow, framing her Caucasian face. She looks almost like a sleeping princess, and I feel bad at having to wake her. I'm surprised she's sleeping through Naga and Elan's chomping, although the sound probably wasn't as loud inside. The thumping probably woke me because my nerves are still on edge after having been trapped in the wretched realm of Muspelheim.

Shaking her shoulder lightly, I call her name. "Eir. I'm sorry to wake you, but we have to get up and have breakfast before our teacher comes barging in."

She stretches her arm beyond the pillow,

connecting softly with the wall before groaning and arching her back. "Is it morning already?"

"Yes, it's morning, and Elan and Naga are already having breakfast. We better have ours before we miss out and have to train." I place a hand over my warbling stomach. "I'd hate to train on an empty stomach. It's so hard to concentrate, and I get a little cranky."

She's telling the truth. You don't want to see that side of her.

I glare between a crack in the curtains, meeting Elan's amused golden eye.

Eir chuckles lightly. "Well then, we better get you to the dining hall." Pushing herself up, she sits gracefully and hangs her legs over the edge of her bed until her bare feet hit the floor. Her cotton nightie's long sleeves drape around her arms, and the skirt falls to her knees as she stands.

We change into the dresses we wore yesterday, and I run my hands over the fabric, attempting to get used to the looseness and brushing against my skin rather than the tight fighting leathers I usually wear. "I feel strangely more feminine in these clothes."

"Isn't it wonderful?" Eir asks.

I rub the long fabric sleeve down my arm. "To be honest, it's a little daunting. The fabric rubs strangely against my skin and legs. Not only that, it seems to have a softening effect on my fighting attitude."

Breakfast is much the same setup as the dinner, apart from the contents being not as heavy. Many fruits and nuts cover the tables, along with blueberry pancakes and muffins. The assortment looks delicious, yet now that I'm here, my nerves fire through my stomach, dampening my hunger with a blanket of worry.

Eir nudges me gently with her arm. "How come you're not eating? After what you said about getting grumpy if you don't eat, I thought you would be digging into this food."

My shoulders slump, and I stare at the untouched blueberry pancake on my plate. "Yeah. Me too. But ever since I set foot in this dining hall, surrounded by these elves, I find my nervousness rising." I pick up my fork and stab at the pancake. "What if I can't do what they expect me to be able to do?"

Eir studies my face. "What do you mean?"

I drop my fork, and the metal clatters against the crockery plate. "Perhaps my magic is only simplistic, and I can only do simple things, and that's why it hasn't grown over the years—not because I haven't had the correct coaching."

Eir rubs me across my upper shoulders with her hand. "That's ridiculous! You're going to do great!"

I pull my focus away from my plate and look at her. Light and enthusiasm fill her eyes, highlighting her beauty and making her face even more stunning. "I can't wait to practice some more." When she gazes into my eyes, she seems to see my concern, and her expression changes. "Aren't you excited?"

I feign a smile that I know doesn't reach my eyes, and I rub my stomach, attempting to settle the stirring. "I'm just nervous, I think."

"Over what?"

"I guess, after achieving so much a couple of years ago, I'm nervous I'll let everyone down and struggle to learn the magic Aymar is going to teach me."

She lightly squeezes my hand, which rests on the table. "You'll be fine, Kara. Your magic is stronger than mine. If I can learn what I did without a teacher, then you'll do fine."

While attempting to make my smile bigger and more convincing, I swallow the lump blocking my throat. "We'll see." I fork a couple of bits of pancake into my mouth, chew until it's small enough to pass the lump, then grab some berries to eat later and leave the table with Eir following me.

As we approach the cottage, a shadow emerges from a corner. Aymar shifts in front of our door, spotting us at the same time.

He charges toward us, pushing his long sleeves up, revealing his chubby arms. "Ah, there you are. I was starting to think you took off."

"We had to get breakfast." Eir's eyebrows rise as she glances at his broad belly. "I'm surprised we didn't see you there."

He grins and waves a dismissive hand at her. "Don't worry your pretty little face over me. I got in early. It's what I normally do. I have to get all the good food." He winks.

I scratch my head. "I thought the food is replenishable."

His smirk broadens. "It is."

I frown, not quite getting his meaning.

When he spots my confusion, he chuckles and explains. "That means I get the best food more than once."

A shadow streaks low, heading toward me, and I duck right as a colorful zmey flies overhead, narrowly missing me with its claws.

Aymar turns and spots me squatting close to the ground, and he laughs. "Oh, Vanir! You're a magnet for a zmey."

My jaw drops in shock over his amusement, and I frown, unimpressed. "Why would a zmey come after me now?"

"I guess it's making sure you're magically

blessed." He surveys me in a taunting manner, amusement plastered over his face. "Maybe this zmey doesn't know that you've been marked or thinks that you need more markings. It must know that you're new to our realm and wants to double mark you."

Even though the magic doesn't throb in my scar anymore, I rub the shoulder where Loki, shaped like a zmey, marked me approximately four years ago. I frown. "I still don't get it."

"A zmey can mark its target several times. Each time, you can be infused with more magic, causing your magic to grow slightly stronger." He purses his lips and taps a finger on them. "Although that's a rather painful process. Personally, I would suggest more practice to make your magic stronger."

I study the sky through the trees, searching for the zmey as I prepare for another attack.

"Come." Aymar distracts me from my search. "Let's go to the training area. It's under more shelter."

Quickly, I place the bowl of berries on our cottage table, and we follow Aymar through the under-growth of thicker trees into a smaller area almost like an outdoor chapel. Long draping vines are strung from one side to the other, creating a natural cover like the one above the dining hall. Each vine is covered in emerald green leaves and pale-lilac flowers. The strong floral scent floats through the air and calms my nerves. Several vines drape toward the ground at the sides, giving the impression of walls made from nature.

A satisfied sigh escapes Aymar. "This is a nice, secluded place to teach people. I like to bring my students here regularly."

Pacing to the far end of the sheltered area, he circles a hand, creating something in his palm, his back facing us.

Quickly he says, "Think fast!" Within a flash, he spins, releasing several rocks directly at my head.

Astonished shock seizes my muscles. It takes a split second to crack the hold, allowing me to move. Clasping my necklace in one hand, I throw up my free palm, blocking the rocks. A satisfied smile creeps onto my face as they slam into my invisible magic barrier and slide down the front, dropping to the ground.

"Good. You do keep your little magic necklace charged." He twirls his hand, and the rocks on the ground are flung to the side, out of the shelter. "But we have to teach you how to gather your magic instantly so you don't have to rely on what is stored in your necklace."

Mischief dances in his eyes, and I remain alert,

ready for another swift attack. Only a few moments have passed since we arrived in our classroom, yet I can tell he's going to be an interesting teacher.

Chapter Eight

A large rock flies my way, seeming to appear out of nowhere. Palm open, I push toward it with one arm and grasp my necklace with the other, but the magic doesn't come. I haven't recharged my necklace with magic after the last rock flew at me. Aymar hasn't given me time. My cheeks turn clammy as a realization sinks in—I don't have any magic gathered to disperse this large rock aimed straight for my head. I attempt to move away without success, my feet stuck to the spot. Twisting, I turn my upper back toward the careening rock, bracing myself for the impact and the onslaught of pain. After a loud pop, my back and legs are showered with many smaller stones, the impact sharp and strong enough to leave bruises, but I feel nothing else.

As I pull myself out of the cringe, Eir stands beside me with her palms raised and her face set in determination, her eyes sparkling with annoyance directed at Aymar. "You know, I'm all for learning on the spot, but you could at least teach Kara how to conjure her magic quickly before throwing large boulders at her."

I blink at the irritation on Eir's face. Seeing anything but peace in her expression is rare.

Amusement dances in Aymar's eyes. "Of course." He bows mockingly to Eir. "Although that was a test for both of you. It's good to know that you can get angry when it's called for."

Eir lowers her hands, realization covering her face, and her annoyance softens. "I will always defend my friends, and if that calls for anger, then I will thrive on it."

"Good to know." A sly smile creeps onto his face.

Eir's eyebrows push together. "Why are you using rocks in such a violent manner anyway? I thought you were a peaceful magic teacher."

Aymar waves his hands extravagantly wide. "I was testing out what you've learned already. Just because I'm a light elf, it doesn't mean that I can't do dark magic. It's just we prefer not to."

Finally, overcoming my shock, I cross my arms over my chest. "Couldn't you just ask us?"

His sly smile disappears from his face, and he holds up both hands in a stopping motion. "Alas, I will only use light magic on you from now on. I apologize if I upset you."

My resolve wavers, and my arms fall to my side. "You didn't offend me. I just wasn't expecting this behavior from a light elf, and as Eir said, it would be nice if you trained me how to pull from my magic instantly and not have to store it or let it build before I can use it."

"Ha." Aymar claps his hands once then spreads his arms wide, the smile returning to his face. "Of course." He paces quickly for a large being, and before I know it, he is by my side, placing a palm on my forehead. "I think it best if I show you rather than slowly explaining the process."

The instructions play visually in my mind, and I instantly put the instructions to use. My body feels strangely charged, ready to release the magical energy when needed. By the time he has shown Eir the instructions, my nerve endings are firing. I wrap my hand around the pendant hanging from my necklace and offload the explosive edge of magic into the stone's storage.

Aymar's eyebrow rises. "Good thinking. You should never need the excess magic, but it's best to have a backup plan just in case something happens." He turns to Eir. "How are you feeling?"

She blinks a couple of times, her expression blank

as she attempts to process the information he's just inserted into her. "Fine. I think I've got it." She shakes out her shoulders.

He nods approvingly. "Good. Now you are both ready to start practicing."

Suddenly, another large rock about half the size of my body appears out of nowhere, aiming straight for my torso. In the time it takes to blink, I raise my hands and shoot magic at the boulder, shattering it into hundreds of little pieces.

"Ha ha. Fantastic! Do you see how much quicker it is, learning that way?"

Dumbfounded, I blink slowly and nod. "Does this mean that you are going to teach us everything this way?"

He scoffs, waving a dismissive hand at me. "Of course not. Some things I will, but sometimes, it is more fun to learn things the long way." Glancing down at the shattered mess, he says, "Now, put this back together."

I do as instructed.

Aymar circles the boulder sitting on the ground a couple of feet away. "Good. Now, I want you to demolish and construct this boulder several times."

Even though it reminds me of the times I trained with Gilroma, doing exercises like this, I follow his instructions, hoping that if I do, he will teach us new things soon. I repeat the process several times, shielding myself and the others with a magic barrier every time the boulder shatters. Occasionally, shards nick my skin, and I apply the healing magic Anita taught me. While I practice this exercise, Eir completes several little magic tricks, including the one she already knows, holding and caring for a flame on her palm.

Aymar watches with interest and doesn't seem surprised at what Eir can do, even though it's something she learned from studying books in the academy library. He isn't teaching us anything new, only increasing the speed at which we can pull from our magic. From the corner of my eye, I watch with awe as Eir performs the tricks she taught herself. Having been kept so busy running after Thor over the last couple of years, I haven't had much time to study. When I have, the only books I knew were capable of teaching me magic were in Gilroma's cave and written in Elven, a language I didn't understand.

I intended to learn the language, but I haven't been able to study anything since that day in Gilroma's cave because I haven't stopped since the lava monster attacked Elan at the tunnel's entrance. I've been either running from monsters or chasing leads to recapture Loki. Watching Eir performing her tricks almost makes me envious. The light dancing on the palm of her hand came in handy when we needed it the most.

"Fantastic." Aymar chuckles, his chubby cheeks spread wide with satisfaction.

I stare at him. "What is?"

"What you are both achieving. Now, I want you to learn what Eir is doing, and Eir can learn what you were doing."

"Oh. I already know how to smash rocks and put them back together again." Eir almost sounds disappointed. "When are you going to be teaching us something new?"

Shoving his hands the wrong way up his sleeves, he clasps his forearms. "Soon. It won't be too much longer. I just want to see how much you both know before continuing your instruction. Seeing you already know the rock tricks, I'll get you to teach Kara how to do your little tricks."

As expected, Eir turns out to be the most patient teacher, describing everything perfectly, making it easy to picture the necessary techniques in my mind. Soon, I am balancing flames on my palms and learning how to do simple, harmless magic tricks.

A snap of the fingers pulls my attention away from my practice, and I find Aymar balancing a large platter of food on his hand, picking at small pieces of food and tossing them into his mouth.

I gawk at him. "I can't believe you're eating again."

He chuckles. "My dear, when you work as hard as me, it's important to replenish the body." He shrugs. "Besides, when it's so easy to click your fingers and get any food you want, why wouldn't you?" He conjures a chair and sits on it, platter still in hand. "Why don't you try?"

I shove my hands onto my hips, and my mouth drops open. "Um, because I'm not hungry."

Eir scoffs. "Ignore her. I would love to learn. Who knows when we might need it?" She eyes me curiously from under a raised eyebrow. "And I'm sure you could've used the trick when you were trapped on Muspelheim."

Her comment cuts to my core, and I drop my hands. "You're right. Let's do this. I'm not mocking the magic—I just can't believe you're hungry again."

Aymar shoves more food into his mouth and mumbles, "I'm always hungry."

I push my lips to one side then say, "I'm starting to see that."

Eir circles the platter resting on Aymar's hand, her eyes tracing every detail. "How do we do this?"

He shoves a small pastry filled with custard into his mouth and speaks with his mouth full again. "All you to have to do is envision it."

He spins and places his plate on a nearby bench. I'm surprised he's strong enough to pull his hands away from food in his vicinity long enough to teach us something new. As though reading my thoughts, he suddenly grabs a small tart topped with a cherry from the platter and pops it into his mouth. I roll my eyes then focus on what he is showing us rather than his sloppy eating habits.

He holds out his hands, palms up, as though he is expecting something. "All you have to do is envision it entirely, and it will appear."

I scoff. "I've imagined food many times in my hands when I needed it, but it's never been there."

Aymar approaches, and with a clawlike hand, he touches my abdomen just below my sternum. "You have to feel it from deep within, feel the magic churning, and feel the want strongly enough to make it possible. Imagine what you want to receive in your palm and believe in it."

He moves away yet remains in front of me, again holding out his hands as though ready to accept something. He closes his eyes briefly, and another large platter covered in finger foods of all kinds lands on his raised palm.

He cracks open an eye, briefly glancing at the tray then at me. "It's your turn."

Not feeling very hungry, I decide to picture the

fruit I tasted yesterday afternoon before I fell asleep on the bed. Closing my eyes to focus, I relive the taste, remembering its juiciness and how it tasted like nothing I've eaten on Asgard. As I am conjuring only one piece of fruit, I don't need a plate. Something presses against the soft flesh of my fingertips. Hesitantly, as though too scared to find out if I have conjured the right thing, I pry one eye open. My heart skips with joy, and my second eye flies open when I see the fruit I was hoping for. I prop it on my fingertips and twist my hand in a circle, admiring my handiwork. The fruit is in perfect condition, not a single mark on its flesh.

A strange look crosses the light elf's face as he studies the contents of my hand. "Is that what you wanted?"

"It's what I imagined." I frown at his expression. "Why do you look disappointed? Did I do it wrong?"

His expression turns blank briefly before it cracks with a laugh. "Did I show my disappointment?"

I nod.

Aymar waves a dismissive hand at me. "Ignore that. It appears you did everything right. It's just that you decided to create fruit when there are so many other delicious things to create."

"I happen to like fruit. And this particular one is not on Asgard."

He reaches over to his platter and grabs a large muffin. "In that case, it looks perfect, but you can be the tester. What does it taste like?" He takes a large mouthful of muffin.

I thought his comment strange, considering how keen he was to eat our fruit in the cabin. I shrug, guessing that he liked it if nothing else was around. Sinking my teeth into the juicy flesh, I almost groan with pleasure when the juices run into my mouth. "It tastes delicious," I mutter through my full mouth, working the fluids thoroughly over my taste buds. When I finally swallow my mouthful, I say, "It's definitely what I wanted."

Eir claps her hands excitedly. "My turn."

The light elf holds up a finger, dampening her excitement before turning back to me. "It'll be your turn soon, Eir. But first, I want to see Kara conjure a drink as well. Food is important, but so is water."

After placing my fruit on the edge of one of Aymar's platters, I straighten. "All right." Holding up a hand, I concentrate as I did before, eyes closed, and imagine a drink of water landing on it. Suddenly, my hand is coated with liquid, and I open my eyes to find water dripping off my fingers. I glance at our trainer in surprise.

Amusement dances in his eyes. "You forgot to conjure the cup to hold it in. If you imagined it inside your mouth, then that might work, if it doesn't splutter everywhere. But next time, remember something to hold the liquid."

Even though I know I'm just learning, my cheeks burn as embarrassment races through me. "I feel so stupid. Of course I need something to hold it in."

Picking up on my embarrassment, Aymar rests a hand on my shoulder. "Don't be so critical of yourself. It's a newbie mistake—nearly everybody does it. You're on the right track. Keep practicing with food and drink while I work with Eir."

I survey the platters he created, still laden with food despite his picking at it. "What are we going to do with all the food?"

He follows my gaze. "We don't have to eat it. The idea is practice. Besides, you can always save it for later."

Envy prickles my skin as I briefly watch Eir create food and drinks easily. "You're a natural, Eir. It's humiliating."

Her smooth face blossoms with understanding as she shakes her head. "No. I'm not. It's just because I've had more practice with light magic than you have. I understand the essence a little more."

Chapter Nine

The day passes quickly as we practice the new form of magic.

Aymar leans over a makeshift table he conjured into the training area to hold the food we're creating. Several of our favorite dishes and desserts cover every part of the flat surface. Our teacher picks up a profiterole and sinks his teeth into its hard chocolate coating. Custard oozes down the side of his mouth, and he wipes it away with his thumb.

"Well, we don't need to visit the dining room. You two have done an excellent job of providing food." Licking his thumb and the edges of his mouth, Aymar again eyes the large display of food with keen interest while rubbing his belly. "If you ever get kidnapped

again—"

I open my mouth to protest, only to pause when he holds up his hand.

He eyes me with a knowing expression. "It's not that I want it to happen again. I'm merely saying if you ever get kidnapped again, you shouldn't go hungry or thirsty."

My stomach rumbles, and I join him at the table. "I always hope it just doesn't happen again. I think I've been abducted more than enough times."

He grabs another sweet, this time a piece of slice, which has a cookie pastry filled with caramel and topped with chocolate. He chuckles, and something about it irks me. "You never know. You're someone who's always getting into trouble." The chocolate topping of the slice cracks softly when he takes a bite. "With your track record, you could end up being abducted again, especially if you work for Thor and attempt to capture Loki." With caramel- and chocolate-covered teeth, he chuckles again, but the laughter is cut short and his eyes widen when vines from the natural ceiling dislodge and wrap around his mouth, halting his slight mockery.

Shocked at why the vines suddenly decided to halt his tongue, I peer at Eir, amused when a broad smile spreads across her face.

"Now, that shut you up." Eir's right hand is poised high, her fingers tracing a circle in the air as the vines obey her instruction to wrap another time around Aymar's mouth. She tuts. "You're not exactly lifting Kara's spirits. After everything she has been through, I would expect a little more understanding from you. I thought light elves were about peace and harmony. It almost sounds like you wish for her to be kidnapped."

Aymar shakes his head, urgency and a keenness to cooperate showing in his eyes. Even though Eir isn't hurting him, he doesn't seem to like being prevented from talking… or eating.

The strange conniving look vanishes from Eir's face, and the regular peaceful expression takes over. With the reversal of her spinning fingers, the vine drops from the elf's mouth and retreats back into the other vines in the ceiling.

Aymar quickly says, "No, I definitely don't wish it on her. I was just saying…" He shrugs, looking sheepish.

Eir's eyes narrow in a final threat to leave me alone. "We don't need you to say anything of the sort."

My heart swells with warmth for my friend. Although I could have just shrugged off what he said as ignorant, having someone stand up for me was nice.

Aymar rubs his face, running his fingers several times over his mouth, fascination replacing his expression of shock. "That's a good job of using your magic." He watches the vines' final retreat. "I haven't even taught you that one, yet you picked it up end executed it naturally."

Eir's expression remains humble. "I've been practicing peaceful magic for a while. I find it easy to connect with the elements and use them as I wish."

Exhaustion seeps into my bones, and I grab a small plate, loading it with meat and salad, and sit on a nearby bench, forking some lettuce into my mouth while I study the food we've created.

"I think that will do for today." Aymar's eyes are almost sympathetic as he studies me. "I can see you're exhausted. You've done well for the first day." He eyes the table of food. "I'm going to help myself to some more food. After that, I have some errands to run." He nudges Eir with an elbow. "Come. Let's eat. This all looks delicious."

He is right. Each morsel I place in my mouth just melts. Even the leaves of the lettuce have the right amount of crispness and taste. If Asgard had this kind of magic, they wouldn't have to harvest so much from Midgard.

Blinking in surprise, I watch our magic teacher pull out a fabric bag and stuff it with all different fruits, meats, and desserts—all the foods that would travel well.

As though sensing my astonishment, he catches

my eye and chuckles. "It's food for the road." He rubs his belly. "You don't expect me to starve, do you?" Without waiting for an answer, he swings the bag over his shoulder and leaves.

Despite the abundance of food, several spots on the table lie bare after it was shamelessly stripped to fill Aymar's bag. Even so, a large amount is left, more than enough for Eir and me. "You know, it's a shame we couldn't bring Hildr and Britta to learn this magic and sample this food. There's enough here for all of us."

"We'll just have to teach them ourselves." She seems to notice my face twisting in anguish over the memory of being exiled from Asgard. "Or if things don't work out as planned, then I'll teach them. Hildr will probably listen now that she sees the benefit of peaceful magic." Eir places a hand on my knee. "We'll get you back to Asgard. You'll see."

My nod is hurried, and I change the subject quickly before tears creep to the surface. "What do you suppose the dragons are doing?"

Eir grabs several pieces of meat on one of the platters, her long flowing blue sleeves tickling the food as she reaches over. "I don't know. As soon as we've finished, we can search for them." Plunking herself next to me on the bench, she says, "I've had enough to eat. We've done well."

Pressing against my knees, I stand and brush my hands down my dress to smooth the fabric. "Me too. Let's go find the dragons."

Leaving the food, we return to our cottage and find the dragons outside. Their eyes are sealed shut, tails tucked around torsos, and heads resting on front talons.

Gently, I push one of Elan's eyelids open a crack. "Elan. Have you been sleeping this whole time?"

Lazily, her eye focuses on me and narrows before she turns her head away to scratch the side of her face with a back talon. *As a matter of fact, we've been flying all day. Now I'm tired.* She curls her body and lowers her head to her talons.

Again my exhaustion rises, and I slide my back down against her stomach and sit within her crescent. "Where did you fly to?"

She yawns. *We traveled north. This realm is beautiful.*

Eir places her platter of meats in front of Naga, which seems to awaken the blue dragon. He stretches his front legs, extending his talons, and sniffs the food. *Naga and Elan traveled very far. Alfheim is beautiful, Eir.* The blue dragon lifts his head and peers dreamily at his rider friend. *When Eir gets time, she needs to discover this place. There is so much beauty. Much better than the dragon wastelands and much pret-*

tier than Asgard. He nips at a piece of meat with his front teeth and swallows it lethargically.

Even though exhaustion racks my body, I have to ask Elan, "Have you had enough to eat today?"

Surprisingly, both Elan and Naga nod.

"Seriously?" I wonder if this is really my dragon because I know the extent of Elan's appetite.

With droopy eyes, she nods. *Seriously. Freyr looked after us. He's given us much to eat. More accurately, he has been a perfect host, at least to us.*

I twist my mouth to one side, unsure how to take the fact that the god is looking after our dragons more than us. "That's nice to hear. I haven't seen him since we arrived."

Elan yawns then smacks her lips together a few times. *How did your lesson go?* Exhaustion muffles her voice.

Reaching up with both my arms, I stretch toward the sky. "For the first day, I think we did well. I'm exhausted from making food all day, but if you're hungry, I'm willing to give it another go. If you're not, then I could certainly save my energy."

Naga wraps his tail loosely around Eir. *Save your energy. Naga and Elan are very full. As Elan said, Freyr treated us well.*

A screech pierces the air, and shivers run down my spine.

"That sounded like a zmey," I whisper.

All eight of our eyes rise to the sky to find our vision is blocked by the thick canopy of leaves. On the one hand, the lack of visibility makes me uneasy. On the other, I hope that also means the creature doesn't know we're here.

"I can't see anything." Eir's voice isn't much more than a whisper.

Another screech sounds closer, stiffening my back like a board as I search the sky. "I can't see anything either."

The leaves rustle not far above my head, and I spin, spotting the colorful creature, careering straight at me through the leaves.

- Chapter Ten -

With a screech, the zmey dives at me. Riddled with exhaustion, I can't think clearly enough to summon my magic to stop it. Large golden feet thump on each side of me, and an enormous form towers above. I catch a glimpse of Elan's golden scales over me as the muscles in her legs ripple with tension. She snarls, deep and low.

As much as I'm enticed by having my magic enhanced, I'm not keen on being scratched again by a zmey. Their markings hurt, not to mention how terrifying the creatures are. I would rather strengthen my magic by practicing.

A twig cracks to my right, and in my peripheral vision, Naga is protecting Eir in the same way, the lower part of his stomach touching her head slightly. He's not as big as Elan, but that doesn't stop him from standing guard. He exposes his broad array of teeth in a snarl—a strange look on the soft-hearted blue dragon. Even a peaceful creature can be protective and nasty when protecting loved ones.

When the zmey nears, both Elan and Naga lurch forward, blocking all passage to us. The creature swerves, and the leaves on the forest floor rustle from the force of its wings. It twists and pushes out through the canopy of branches.

After a few moments, my heart stops thumping profusely in my chest. Despite having a Valkyrie's healing ability, I'm grateful I don't have to go through the pain of one of their scratches again.

Holding a hand over her heart, Eir follows the zmey with her eyes. "That was close. I don't know why, but it seems to be targeting us."

Confusion washes over me, and I rub my forehead with the back of one hand, watching the zmey disappear. "Maybe it's Loki causing more mischief." I drop my arm by my side. "I have no idea why it was going for us."

Elan shifts from towering over me and sits on her haunches. *What makes you think it was Loki?*

Sliding one hand up a loose sleeve, I play with the point of my elbow. "I don't know. I don't know where he is. I guess I automatically assume everything that causes mischief has to be Loki in a shifter form. He's roaming somewhere, and he could be doing anything."

Eir leans against Naga's front leg, resting her head against his scales. "I'm too exhausted to keep going. I'm going to get some sleep and, hopefully, feel refreshed in the morning."

Placing my palm on Elan's nose, I rub it softly. "Me too. I'll see you in the morning."

As we make our way to the cabin, we're followed by the sounds of crackling leaves and snapping twigs as the two dragons make themselves comfortable again. We're so tired that the lightness remaining in the sky doesn't concern us as we tuck ourselves into bed. Very soon, my exhaustion melts off my shoulders and back and seeps into the mattress.

A strange sound pulls me from my sleep. The loud chirping of birds sounds from outside, and I pry my eyes open, peering around a room filled with light. I'm not sure if I've slept all night or if I had a few minutes' nap, but my body has the same feeling after a good night's rest, and by the enthusiastic sounds of the birds, I assume morning has come. After throwing back my white sheets, I drape my feet over the edge of my bed, untangling them from the long cotton nightwear. The strange feeling of loose fabric rubbing against my legs follows me to the window. I fling back the curtains and peer into the forest. The two dragons are nowhere to be found.

Eir's sleepy voice sounds from her bed. "What is

it?" She rubs the sleep out of her eyes, slowly pushing herself up to sit.

I swipe my long brunette hair over one shoulder. "I thought I heard something, and I can't see the dragons outside."

She stands, and her nightie drapes to the ground, the soft fabric caressing her curves as she joins me to peer out the window. "They've probably gone for a flight. Most likely, they think we'll be training all day, and they've gone searching for some entertainment." She stretches her arms to the ceiling and sways her hips from side to side. Then she heads to the drawers and pulls out a pale-green gown and lays it on her bed. "I guess we should get ready for today's lesson. I would imagine Aymar is back from whatever errand he had to run yesterday." After returning to the drawer, she holds up a pale-blue gown in my direction, stringing it between her hands. "Are you happy with this one? I think it would look lovely with your brunette hair."

I take it from her. "It will do. Thanks. I'm still not used to all these dresses."

A knowing smile crosses Eir's face. "Enjoy it while you can."

After getting changed and slipping on another pair of floral sandals, I follow Eir out of the cabin.

"Do you know what we're supposed to do every day?"

"What do you mean?"

"Our schedule here hasn't been laid out clearly for us. Are we supposed to be training every day, or are there other activities we should be partaking in? Have you heard any more? It's almost like they run on their own time here."

Eir's understanding smile returns. "It's completely the opposite of the academy."

"Exactly!"

"I think it's kind of nice. It's relaxing and peaceful—something we haven't felt for a long time. Even after the academy, we're always training to fight, battling something, or reaping souls."

A small pang of jealousy rips through me. To go out reaping souls for Valhalla was my lifelong dream. After a lot of influencing, I managed to convince Odin to give the wingless Valkyries that ability. It was only possible if Odin had blessed us with the gift. The irony hasn't escaped me that my lifelong dream is something I haven't used while serving under Thor. Although that is an honor, not partaking in the Valkyries' primary function is hard for me to deal with. At least my wingless comrades are now able to reap souls.

After breakfast, Eir and I head toward the little

area we trained under yesterday. Food is scattered across the table, appearing to have been ravaged by wild animals.

With a quick swipe of her hand, Eir makes the food disappear. "I wonder where he is?" Her nose screws up as she eyes the bare table. "I'm kind of shocked that he didn't return and grab more food. I haven't seen anyone like food as much as him."

I push my mouth to one side. "I don't know. Thor would be a close contender."

"True. But Thor would burn it off with all the training he does."

Sitting down on the bench seat, I conjure some blueberries and nibble on them one at a time. When I clamp my teeth on each one, the firm skin pops, and the soft juicy flesh spreads across my tongue. These berries have become one of my favorites.

Eir joins me on the seat, helping herself to my berries as we wait for Aymar to show. Time ticks by slowly, and we wait until our backsides turn numb on the hard bench.

I stand to walk out the numbness. "To me, it feels as though we've waited for him long enough. What do you think?"

Leaving the bench, Eir swings her hips from one side to the other in exaggerated stretches. "I'm starting to think he's not going to come. Maybe we should discover some of the realm. I could use a harmless adventure, and the dragons appear to be impressed. I think it would be nice to see something other than the little village."

"Should we search for the dragons first?"

Her long brown hair tosses around her shoulders as she shakes her head. "Unless you really want to. They seem to be having fun alone. We could go discovering by ourselves. Everybody we've run into in this realm has been friendly." She lifts an eyebrow. "Besides, if we happen to run into any trouble, I think you and I know how to defend ourselves, even without a big, bad dragon towering over us."

I nod, knowing she's right. "Let's walk through the village first in case we just missed Aymar."

Passing through the village center, we observe many elves of all different shapes and sizes going about their daily tasks. Their pace is slow, lacking the urgency of life on Asgard, which makes our realm seem more intense and loaded with pressure. That never struck me before, although the fact didn't make Asgard less enjoyable.

Freyr is nowhere to be seen, and no one stops us as we pass through the village and exit the other side. Trees press in from all sides as we leave civilization and head farther into the forest.

Eir gazes over her shoulder at the village. "These

elves are so peaceful it's unusual. Because of it, everything seems safe, like there can't be anything dangerous nearby. They all seem so casual, without a single worry."

"I have heard that there are dark elves here somewhere, though. It's hard to believe those elves came from the same make and decided to turn dark instead. All those elves that invaded Asgard are from this realm," I said in warning.

"I know. It's hard to believe that they also live here. It seems too peaceful. They must live in a separate part of the realm, away from the light elves. Otherwise, you would think it would affect the peacefulness of the light elves."

As we step through the forest, the trees become more beautiful. Birds sing in the branches, and the leaves rustling in the wind are almost mesmerizing.

Eir releases a satisfied sigh, throwing her head back and closing her eyes. "I could fall in love with this sound."

We wander deeper into the forest, each step more peaceful than the last, pushing away any belief that dark elves live in this realm. The thundering of a waterfall grows louder until we eventually approach a decent-sized mountain. Water cascades down each side into a large lake below and bubbles over rocks as it flows down as a river.

Something splashes in the pool, and I stand at its edge, leaning over to try to get a better view. Eir joins me, and the water ripples in front of us. Something pale darts through the water too quickly for us to focus on it. It circles and creeps closer to the surface, seeming as large as a medium-sized fish. The closer it revolves toward the surface, the sharper it becomes. Yet I still can't see it clearly. A school of small fish travels over the rocks in the shallow water, and the little creature flicks its tail and careers straight through them, plucking a fish from the school. If my eyes are picking it up correctly, it has wings and pale lilac scales with a long tail, and its speed in the water is remarkable.

With my attention focused on whatever the creature is in the water, I start as hands grip me from behind, grabbing my upper arms and dragging me from the water's edge. With wide eyes, I struggle, catching sight of someone else grasping Eir and doing the same.

Chapter Eleven

I wriggle and squirm, slipping in the floral sandals, my feet landing in the water. Instead of helping, my open shoes turn slippery, causing me to miss my Valkyrie boots. Staying upright becomes a struggle, made worse as water soaks my gown's long fabric. The material wraps around my ankles, further constricting my movement.

The mystery creature in the water scurries away, and blood drains from my face when I gaze over my shoulder. Dark elves have grasped us, with several others lining the forest. Even if I manage to battle these ridiculous clothes and escape the elf clasping me, I'll have to fight my way through several others to escape. After having spent some time with the light elves, I can see the similarities, except these elves are more brooding, the light and peacefulness absent. Sinister glints sparkle in their eyes as they drag us from the water's edge, flailing and digging in our heels, our shoes left behind on the bank. Several more hands assist our captors.

Through clamped teeth, I scream. "What do you want?" I stamp a heel, aiming for the elf's toes. It connects with the elf's boot tip with little effect, and my longing for my Valkyrie boots grows.

The long, wet fabric seems to constrict my legs further as I struggle, and a chuckle, low and sinister, ripples through the air when I groan my frustration.

"No amount of wriggling is going to help, Valkyries. You aren't going to escape this many."

Twisting, I search for the face behind the voice, unable to pinpoint the owner. "What makes you think we're Valkyries?"

The elf scoffs. "Do you really think we're that naïve or we don't recognize you?" The sinister laugh returns, making my skin crawl.

My search finally turns fruitful when I catch sight of the cheekbone of one of the elves clasping me.

"We'd recognize you anywhere. You're the Valkyrie that caused so much trouble when we invaded Asgard."

I frown. The dark elf leader from that day is dead. Twisting farther, I finally catch sight of the elf taunting me. He's unfamiliar.

I try again to insert some hesitation into his resolve. "What makes you think that I'm that

Valkyrie? The battle took place so long ago. How could you possibly remember with certainty that I'm that Valkyrie?"

He binds my hands together with a long rope. "The image of your face is embedded in my mind." Evil, slimy tones weave through his words. "I made sure I remembered your face, waiting for the day that I would find you, knowing I would persecute you if I had the opportunity."

I struggle, whipping my arms from side to side, but to no avail. My minimal cover is blown, eliminating any rationale for denying it. Eir's face is ghostly white as she remains secured between two elves.

I stop struggling. "Let my friend go. She had nothing to do with it. It's all my doing."

The elf's eyes set in determination as he shakes his head. "She's your friend, so she had something to do with that."

My brow bunches. "But she wasn't even there. Your leader made her disappear somewhere. She wasn't at the battle."

His mouth lifts in a sly smile. "That may be so. But I'm sure she would've been there if she could. That makes her just as guilty as you."

I flash Eir a sorrowful look. She shakes her head. Even in this situation, she looks peaceful. The older she gets, the less she seems to experience stress, and I wonder how she does it. Even so, I mentally reprimand myself. I feel responsible even though it isn't my fault. If she weren't my friend, she wouldn't be in this situation, yet her eyes hold me blameless.

The dark elves march us away from the water's edge, pushing us forward into the forest in the opposite direction of Freyr's village, Yantolos. The forest thickens, and an eerie quiet creeps between its branches—the forest's thickness is broken occasionally by mountains. They march us through the mountains and into crevices, leading us into a dark, dingy cave below the earth. Water drips down the walls, pooling frequently, and falling drops echo through the stone enclosure.

The confined path leads farther underground. Burning sconces line the wall, lighting the way through the caves, which mesh into one another. The farther we travel, the more the caves remind me of Gilroma's magic-made cave, although that cave had less water seeping down the walls. With each additional room, the atmosphere seems to change, blanketing me with dreary darkness that seems to creep into my soul.

We pass several other elves, cloaked in dark, form-fitting clothes similar to fighting leathers, casting us with an unwelcoming glare. These long, flowing, pale gowns of the light elves couldn't be more out of place. We look like we are their enemies, the light elves, not just detested Valkyries. My unease grows with each step. At least the wet hem is finally starting to dry out, easing the uncomfortable rubbing around my calves.

The connecting rooms eventually reach a large open area where different paths join in one communal area.

As I catch Eir's gaze, her uneasiness reflects my own as the elves push us into the open. "Where are you taking us?"

Amusement crosses the leader's face, and he yanks at the rope tied around my wrist. "You ask like you have a choice. You're prisoners. We're taking you to where we can hold you. You won't be able to escape from this area. As you can see, there are many of us down here, and you stand out like sore thumbs." He tugs at the rope securing my wrists, which draws me closer. I can feel dark magic whirling underneath his skin. It's a strange and new sensation for me, almost as though my magic senses have awakened since I've come here.

We reach the center of the open community area, passing women, children, and men, almost all sets of eyes staring at us. The hall isn't crowded, but one thing is certain—too many eyes are in here, preventing an escape, especially in a dress like this.

An annoying satisfaction laces the elf's voice. "As you can see, there are many elves in here. They have all had an image of your face plastered inside their memories. I have shared it with the group. You'll never be able to escape from here. Someone will recognize you instantly." He travels down a hallway and passes several more rooms hewn from the stone. We pass an indoor waterfall and weave deeper underground past many corridors until we eventually arrive at a dark, dingy area. With a wave of our captor's hand, the stone doorway slides across, and he shoves us inside with such force that we struggle to stay on our feet.

The stone-walled room is tiny. We would be lucky to stretch out flat on the ground to sleep without our heads and feet touching both walls. One sconce burns on a wall, illuminating the dark ceiling about two feet above. Just looking around this tiny enclosure is enough to send someone over the edge. It's claustrophobic, and not a window is in sight. I already miss being in nature. Other than being smaller, it reminds me of the cave where the gods held Loki prisoner, tied up wearing a loincloth and a snake dripping searing venom onto his bare skin. The thought of that horrible torture sends a shiver down my spine, dampened only by the knowledge that I helped release him from that, even if that was an accident.

The stone door slams shut behind us, and I call after them, banging my palm on the door. "Wait!"

Boots clicking on the stone floor, slowly fading, is my answer. They've left us all alone in this horrible enclosure.

Chapter Twelve

After thumping the stone door a few more times, I stop and let the cold silence fill the tiny room. Our breathing reverberates off the walls, the noise sounding like it's being broadcast through a Dictaphone.

Eir runs her fingers over a wall, her peaceful face tainted slightly with worry. Dread plunges a dagger into my heart. I can't believe I'm in this situation again. *This is getting ridiculous.* I pace the room, accidentally knocking Eir's shoulder in the tiny space. This time, I'm not going to be a victim. The dark elves may have captured us for a while, but they're not going to keep us here. The problem lies with the many elves that would stop us along the way.

The soft material flowing around my legs once again reminds me how awkward I feel and how I long for my fighting leathers. Yesterday's lesson springs into my memory, inserting an idea. Surely, I can use that same food-conjuring spell to help change our garments. I focus hard, imagining every layer of my fighting leathers and wishing them to replace my elven gown. Magic whirls around me, overwhelming my senses. For a brief moment, a magical tornado whips around me, dying after a few moments and bringing a more familiar sensation. Comfort embraces my skin, and when I peek down at my body, my heart jumps with joy. I'm wearing my black fighting leathers, not a rip or a spot of dirt from Muspelheim showing. Suddenly, each movement feels familiar and comfortable, with no constricting fabric getting in the way.

"Fantastic!" Pride fills Eir's voice as I beam at her. "You've already transformed the magic you learned to make food." She brushes her pale gown with her hands. "I also feel ridiculous in this gown. Can you do the same for me?"

Focusing and replacing her soft gown with the Asgardian fighting leathers she would typically wear takes only a few moments.

Her eyes shine with excitement. "Thanks. I could have done that myself, but I wanted you to get some more practice. Even if they have our faces planted in their brains, it will be harder for them to process seeing us in these fighting leathers." She brushes a hand down a black sleeve then ties her long brown hair back into a ponytail. "These leather clothes will blend in better with what the dark elves are wearing."

"Maybe so, but first, we need to get out of this cave."

Eir's strange expression causes me to frown. The glint in her eyes grows, and she smirks. "You do remember that you can move rocks, right?"

Grimacing, I slap a palm against my forehead. "Of course. Why am I so stupid at times?"

She rubs my upper arm. "You're not stupid. Sometimes, you just don't think outside of the box when you should."

Harnessing my magic, I focus on moving the rock door aside. The grating of rocks fills the room as the door opens slightly then snaps shut before the gap is wide enough for us to sneak through.

Frowning, I try again—the muscles of my neck strain with tension as I will my magic to force the door open. Though I attempt this several times, it just creates a ruckus each time, the rock grating across the floor slightly then clanking as it slams shut. My nerves fire with frustration, and I know unwanted attention is bound to come our way if this continues.

Eir pushes her lips to one side, her brow creased in thought. "It's playing difficult. There must be a charm around it to stop us from moving the rock aside, at least enough to let us out." Placing a hand on the door, she runs her palm over the surface, trying to sense a counterspell.

After a few minutes, my impatience gets the better of me. "Are you picking up anything?"

She lifts a finger to her lips, and I fall silent. After a short pause, she whispers, "I'm going to insert it with peace to see if I can trick it into opening." Closing her eyes, she wriggles her fingers at the closed door.

With my fingers crossed behind my back, I wait, my anticipation rising, hoping whatever she is doing will work.

Finally, she opens her eyes. "That's it." She steps back and glances over her shoulder at me. "Give it another go."

Sucking in a deep breath, I focus my magic on the door again. It slides open halfway. For a moment, I'm too afraid to move. Maybe what I'm seeing is a trick of the mind. Quickly, I shove that thought aside, grasp Eir's arm, and drag her through the gap with me. The back of my neck is riddled with tension, for I expect the door to slam shut on us at any moment. Thankfully, the door remains open for a short while longer before closing slowly.

"What did you do to the door?" I whisper.

Eir grins, clearly pleased. "I tickled it with magic."

My mouth drops open as I stare at her, confused.

"It's a part of nature. Nature loves peace, so I tickled its edges, reminding it what it's like to be peaceful. It seemed to lap it up. Despite what control the dark elves have placed on it, it wanted to break free." She straightens her shoulders. "Peaceful magic has its place. Magic doesn't all have to be used to defend or attack. It's a good lesson for Hildr to learn."

I shake my head. "Good luck with that. Hildr needs to see the benefit of peaceful magic to believe what you just said."

Our eyes peeled, we quietly make our way through the stone halls, trying to remember the way the dark elves brought us. Even though we've changed into our dark leather uniforms, we stick to the shadows. We tiptoe in our boots, attempting to quiet the heels clacking on the rocks.

We reach a small group of elves sitting in one of the rock-built rooms we have to pass through. Eir and I make eye contact, a silent agreement passing between us. We make sure our ears' tips are hiding under our hair and straighten our shoulders, walking through the room as though we belong. My heart jumps to my throat as the elves briefly look up then return to what they are doing. One elf is rocking a screaming baby in her arms, covering part of its face with a cloth to block out the light from a nearby sconce. Her attention is too focused on calming the baby to worry about us. Just to be safe, we keep our faces to the front and hide behind our hair.

A mustiness thickens the air as an indoor waterfall's trickling grows louder, drowning the noise of our boots. We follow large stepping stones across the underground river, taking us to the other side. Several corridors branch out from the main room, and we try to remember the way the elves brought us. Eir tilts her head in the direction of the passage on the right, and I follow her lead.

The corridor narrows just before we turn a corner to find the way lined by another group of elves. Keeping my head down, I scan their faces, searching for any sign that they recognize us. My feet falter when I catch sight of the elf that took the lead in locking us away. My heart races as I attempt to cover my mistake, only to run into Eir, who halts momentarily on the path. Instantly, every set of eyes lands on us.

Chapter Thirteen

Instinctively, I reach for the cave wall, grasping for its firmness in an attempt to stop my head from spinning. Missing the wall, I wobble sideways and stumble into a small space hidden by the darkness.

As my arms flail, searching for the wall's solidness, something grasps me around a wrist, yanking me sideways into the gap. Rocks clatter as I stagger into the darkness, barely making it between the two rock surfaces on either side. Eir gasps and clasps me, dragged along behind. The clacking of rocks colliding behind us draws my attention in time to see the dim light of the corridor disappearing as the rocks slam together, illuminating the final crack. Suddenly, the space feels more claustrophobic than the little room the elf had trapped us in.

Something continues to yank me along sideways,

and my feet trip over rocks lining the floor, seeming to find every ridge along its dark surface. Stones rub along my back and front, sometimes barely allowing enough space for me to slide through. The clasp of Eir's hand remains firm around my wrist even as she struggles to weave her thin frame through the gap.

Darkness completely encases us, and after a few minutes of being dragged through this rocky hell, I still don't know who our new captor is. No amount of searching gives away whatever or whoever is pulling us along. All that I know is they certainly have a firm grasp. Only hope keeps me going—hope that whatever this is doesn't have ill intentions toward us.

After a little more stumbling, a soft hiss seizes my attention, similar to the sound Elan makes when she is shooting a plume of fire, only quieter. A ball of glowing orange captures my vision, illuminating the tiny face of a creature.

I blink in an attempt to wipe away the trick my eyes are playing on me. A tiny creature sits on the arm of our captor. A small flame dances on the captor's palm, bringing with it a dim light illuminating the outline of the thing dragging us. My body stiffens. It's a dark elf, and on her arm sits a tiny lilac dragon. The dragon flicks its spiked tail over the elf's arm and runs up to her thin shoulders to wrap its body around her slender neck, which is covered in black leather zipped up to her chin, pointing its tiny face our way.

The elf pauses then twists, her black leather squeaking as it catches on a rock. Pointy ears stick out from under wavy shoulder-length brunette hair with silver streaks. Even in the orange glow of the flame, her face is pale as though she rarely sees the sun.

When her dark almond-shaped eyes land on me, I suck in a quick breath and scowl. "What do you want from us?"

Her dark lips purse, emphasizing her hollow cheekbones. "Is that what I get for saving you?"

"Is that what you're doing?"

Eir releases me from her grasp and moves closer, leaning over my shoulder. "Not that we're not grateful."

Feeling bad for my tardiness, I add, "I didn't know what you were doing."

The young elf's expression doesn't show any emotion, and despite having just done us a favor, she speaks in a monotone. "I'm saving you from the group."

I eye the little dragon curiously. "Thank you."

"Why would you want to save us?" Eir asks.

The elf's eyes narrow on Eir. "Am I not allowed to save whomever I please? I thought you of all people, being the peaceful one, would understand that."

"Oh, I understand it," Eir says. "But excuse my ignorance. On Asgard, it's believed that all dark elves are only for themselves and live to harm."

A strange smirk crosses the dark elf's face. "That is true. Mostly. But I have someone who wanted me to do it."

I frown. "Who?"

The little dragon circles her shoulder and returns to where it was curled. The strange lilac scales glow in the small flame's orange light, and its big lilac eyes study Eir then me, its tongue licking one eye then the other.

Eir reaches for the little creature and stops midway. "Is that truly a little dragon?"

"Yeah. It's a dragon." The elf sounds disinterested. "That's what it is."

The little dragon continues licking its eyes alternately, stretching its tongue and circling it around the flame on the elf's hand. Twirling its tongue, with the flame on top, it embraces the orange light and douses it before it reaches its mouth.

I gasp. "What just happened?"

The elf releases an amused grunt. "Meet Zildryss. This little guy is the reason why I'm here."

"What do you mean?" I ask, wishing the fire was still burning so I could see the elf's expression.

"For some reason, this little guy wanted me to rescue you. So here I am." She doesn't sound too impressed about helping us, and not seeing her is making me nervous.

"Can we have the flame back, please?"

"Zildryss. Give them back the flame. They want to see us."

A small ball of flame exits the dragon's tiny mouth, seeming attached to his tongue as it rolls out like a carpet.

Eir places her palm up, resting the back of her hand on my shoulder. The flame skips across the small void and onto her hand, dancing on her palm. "Thank you." She studies the little dragon. "I've never seen anything like it, even in the books in the academy library."

"That's because they're scarce even on Alfheim. We try to keep their existence a secret and out of any books. For some reason, this little guy has taken a liking to you. He spotted you by the lake before the other dark elves grabbed you."

Realization finally hit me. "That's what was swimming in the water and grabbed a little fish."

The dragon suddenly pushes off her shoulders, flaps its wings, and lands on mine.

I start. "Is he dangerous?"

A sly smirk creeps onto the elf's face. "Define *dangerous.*"

"All right." My eyebrows push together in a frown. "What I mean is will he hurt us?"

He crawls around my shoulders to my chest and peers up at my face, studying me. I'm not entirely sure how to interpret his expressions.

Amusement dances in the elf's dark eyes. "As I said, he seems to have taken a liking to you. That usually means that he's not dangerous—at least, not to you."

The tiny dragon explores me with his eyes, raising a strange kind of self-consciousness. Even seeing the long spikes running down his back, I can't believe this little guy could be dangerous, but this is a different realm, and many things seem strange.

Suddenly, Zildryss flicks his tongue and licks me on a cheek. One thing is sure—his tongue is a lot longer than I thought.

I screw up my nose and look at him with a cocked eyebrow. "Okay. Thanks, little guy."

He scurries over my shoulders, along my neck behind my hair, then springs out with his wings spread to glide toward Eir. After landing on her shoulder, he circles her curiously, checking her face, as he did mine, then the flame in her palm.

Eir chuckles. "You're an interesting creature. I'm always willing to make new friends. So that could include you too."

The little dragon nudges her, rubbing the top of his head against her cheek. She squeals with excitement.

The bored voice of the elf pierces our brief happiness. "Okay, this is all very sweet, but we need to get a move on. Follow me."

I had almost forgotten our enclosed surroundings, just big enough to fit us between the rocks.

She spins and continues away from where they rescued us, heading deeper into the mountain, the walls closing around us, making it hard even for our thin bodies to slide through sideways. The pulling and scraping of leather against the stone follow us every step of the way.

The darkness creeps into my soul, whispering doubt and distrust. I hope the strange elf has good intentions and doesn't lead us to an even more sinister place. I find myself doubting any dark elf would help us even if they say they are doing it because a tiny little dragon wants her to.

When I peer over my shoulder, two big lilac drag-on's eyes are staring at me as Zildryss's tongue wipes from one eye to the other. He almost seems to be smirking at me, and although he's cute, I don't know if this is a good or bad thing. My uneasiness grows, and I can't help wondering if we are being led to something more ominous.

Chapter Fourteen

The rocks press closer, crowding the darkness around us. The dark elf splits Eir's flame in two and beckons half to float onto her hand, lighting the way ahead. Trusting this dark elf is proving difficult, but the enclosing rocks leave no choice. We even have to pivot our hips at certain spots and weave our way through to let our backsides slide past bends in the crack.

With each step forward, the fear of being trapped within these rocks rises.

"It's a good thing we're all thin." I chortle, trying to make light of the situation. When the mysterious dark elf doesn't respond, the worry churning in my stomach deepens, and the claustrophobic smell of damp rock and earth seems to intensify. "Are you sure this leads to something? And that we're not going to be led into a tight spot and trapped?"

She pauses unexpectedly just as I'm concentrating on my next footstep, and I run into her side, feeling the warmth of her body against mine. Instinctively, I jerk back. Her dark eyes land on me, eerily darkened by the shadows of the dull light Eir holds at the rear.

"Sorry," I mutter, feeling the unease growing in my stomach.

Something about her eyes reminds me of Loki. Surely, he wouldn't have shifted into a dark female elf when he already has the dark-elf form of Gilroma. But then, I couldn't know. He's taken on so many forms around me, even the familiar form of Sobek. I'll just have to remain alert and tread carefully with this elf and learn a little more about her, if possible. "What is your name?"

One side of her face rises in a smirk. "Where did that come from?"

"Well…" I stutter, "You're so helpful to us, and I just realized we don't even know your name. We only know the dragon's name."

"I guess that is true. My name is Elaith."

"Thank you for your help, Elaith. I'm K—"

"Kara. Yes. And your friend is Eir."

Confusion races through me. *How does she know?* "Oh. Yes. That's true."

The elf mutters softly, "Zildryss."

Suddenly, the little dragon jumps onto my shoulders and climbs onto my head, his little talons digging into my scalp before he jumps onto the elf's shoulder.

The dark elf smiles and rubs the dragon's cheek with her fingertips. The little lilac dragon tilts his head into the rub then lifts his chin before pressing his other cheek into the elf's fingertips. The elf then weaves her way forward, holding the flame in front of her until she can barely squeeze through the gap.

I groan because she's thinner than me. "How can we get through this?"

"I see your magic instructor hasn't taught you anything useful yet." Her words echo back to me.

My movements falter when her words register. "How did you know we had a magic teacher?" I stare at the back of her silver hair, glowing dimly in Eir's pale light.

Elaith's voice remains nonchalant. "You'd be surprised how much I know."

Zildryss presses into her cheek then circles his long lilac tail, lined with pointy scales along the spine, around the elf's neck. The dark elf's chest heaves, and she waves her hands with palms forward, snuffing the tiny flame out as she pushes and places a palm on each side of the crack. The ground and sides of the crack rumble, and small stones clatter down the thin gap as the two walls shake into a wider position.

My senses charge to full alert as I expect something to drop from above and crush us, but it never comes. Instead, the gap is now wide enough for us to travel in a regular walk.

"How is that possible?" I ask.

The elf turns back, regarding me incredulously. "It's magic you should've learned by now."

"Really? How?"

"Your magic teacher should have taught you, but he probably hasn't because he thinks it to be dark magic."

Eir calls over my shoulder, "How is that dark magic?"

"For some reason, the light elves have decided that moving any kind of earth is dark magic. They think it's bad for the earth."

Eir holds her light over my shoulder, highlighting Elaith's face. "How is it bad for the earth?"

Elaith blocks the light from her eyes with her arm. "They believe it disrupts the earth's natural surface and causes future tremors to rock the crust."

"And what's your opinion?" I ask.

She drops her arm and shrugs, turning to continue through the gap. "I guess you could say it is damaging, but it would have to be done to a certain part."

I keep pace with her. "Like what?"

Rock crunches under our boots as we follow her. Zildryss circles her neck and peers at us through her parted silver hair.

"Like something that holds the stability of the ground. If you're careful, you can move rocks and earth without damaging anything. It's as easy as returning rocks to where they came from or stopping them from falling around you."

I frown. A comment like that doesn't help me eliminate her from the possibility of being Loki. This was a practice I did with Gilroma, who was Loki in a dark elf's form. I swallow, attempting to remove the lump in my throat.

Elaith halts and stares straight at me as though she just read my thoughts. Her eyes seem hollower somehow and her skin paler under Eir's dim light. "But, I must add, moving mountains takes a lot of energy. It's quite draining."

"Can you teach us?" I ask. Whether this is Loki or not, I'm keen to learn more magic.

The side of her mouth rises despite the weariness on her face. "I was intending to teach you a little magic." Her hand runs lightly along Zildryss's tail, bouncing over the points. "It's not something I volunteered. This little guy has insisted that I teach you."

Dumbfounded, I observe the little dragon circling Elaith's neck to face us. The orange glow of the flame taints the lilac of his scales. He puffs out his chest and spreads his short wings, which appear to be broken down into sections the size of feathers, not one membrane strung over the whole wing like large dragons have. At the base of each feather-sized membrane is a blue dot like the eye of a peacock feather. Each membrane is slightly transparent and attaches to a long bone as in a bird's wing.

The dragon's stare almost mesmerizes me, and I'm stuck in his bizarre gaze. "You act like this little guy can speak."

Zildryss tilts his head sideways, and the spikes on his spine stand to attention. At first, this seems threatening, but I realize his little face is more curious than anything else.

Elaith huffs a laugh. "I guess you could say that. But instead of words, the dragon uses images and shows you what he's trying to communicate. You'd be surprised what this dragon can do."

Blinking with disbelief, I stare at the little dragon, caught in his gaze. I can't believe that tiny creature can do much other than looking cute. He sits on shoulders and seems almost childlike, small and harmless.

We progress through the widened passage, which seems to swallow the tiny light on Eir's hand. The way is almost entirely black.

After my thigh collides with a rock protruding from the side, I groan and rub the spot, which will undoubtedly bruise. "We need some more light."

"I'm on it," Eir calls from behind. The flame atop her hand suddenly balloons, throwing out much more light over the rock walls ahead, showing more rocks jutting along our path and even illuminating stones on the ground.

A cracking sound echoes up the space from behind us, and panic fills me. "If you can open paths in the mountain like this, can't the other elves do the same?"

"Some will have magic that can do this, yes. All elves can work magic. It depends on how they have focused their training."

I choke on my saliva and cough. "Well, that doesn't make me feel better."

Elaith calls over her shoulder. "This is why we must hurry. If it helps, the rocks you just heard colliding should have been the ones I sealed when I closed the gap. That way, the other elves can't follow us directly. They should be held up, trying to create a direct path."

The clacking and cracking continue behind us, followed by splitting ahead as our way parts. With this additional worry added to my system, a sudden bout of claustrophobia hits me, and breathing becomes hard in the damp, musty air. Despite having more room around us, I feel trapped, especially with not being able to see the way out. Everywhere we turn, we face more rocks—not a glimmer of natural light anywhere. Through clenched teeth, I suck in the stale air.

As though sensing my distress, Zildryss jumps from Elaith's shoulder and glides to mine, and the little dragon circles my neck, wrapping his belly against my skin. My skin warms, almost to the point of being too hot. Just as I start to touch the dragon to pull him away from my neck, my airway seems to relax, allowing me to breathe more easily.

Elaith pauses and observes the dragon, her eyebrows rising as my expression relaxes. As though sensing his job is complete, Zildryss springs from my shoulders back to Elaith and wraps himself against her skin as though nothing happened.

Elaith runs her fingers down the dragon's spikes and whispers something. Suddenly, the ground shakes, and rocks clatter to the ground. I bend my knees to stabilize myself until the mountain finally stops rumbling.

Elaith glances at us through her silver hair. "Follow me."

A second later, one final crack almost deafens us as the side of the mountain splits. I shield my eyes as a bright light suddenly infiltrates them.

Chapter Fifteen

E ir snuffs out the flame on her hand and walks by me since the path is wide enough for two. The light grows stronger with each step leading us out of the mountain. Trees and foliage cover the edges of the crevice, almost hiding it from any eyes outside. Fresh air fills my lungs as we push through the leaves. Purposefully, I run my fingers over them, ecstatic to feel the give in their fibers.

Zildryss leaps from Elaith's shoulder and lands on mine, circling my neck before jumping onto Eir. Her giggles of delight ring beside me.

She stretches her neck and tilts her face to the sky, stroking his tiny body. "This little guy is so cute. He might even give Naga a run for his money."

"Ooh. Eir, that's pushing your friendship with him." I find it impossible to resist stroking the little dragon and give in to the urge. "They are both adorable. But I can see what you mean. This little guy is tiny, and he has such cute mannerisms."

Zildryss's eyes fix on me, and his long tongue flicks from one eye to the other as though that's a habit when he's processing information about me.

"He has such a long tongue too," I say.

Elaith pauses in front of the last manufactured crack in the mountain and claps her hands—the mountain rumbles as the edges push back together, sealing the hole. "There. No one will know where we came out." Her gaze lands on Zildryss. "That tongue has more purpose than it appears to."

The fresh air is getting to my head and helping me lighten up, inspiring a bad joke. "You mean like eating and tasting." I'm not sure the dark elf gets my humor.

Elaith shoves her fists against her hips. "You may think it strange and mock me, but I'm telling you the tongue does a lot more than that."

Eir tickles Zildryss under the chin. "Like what? The gesture is rather cute."

The impatient scowl on Elaith's face lightens only a little. "Every time that tongue licks one eye and then licks the other one, it is clearing his vision."

Zildryss tilts his head, pushing the top of his crown toward Eir's rubbing fingers.

"Can't he see clearly otherwise?" she asks.

I follow up with "Can't he just blink to clear his eyes?"

As though understanding the conversation, the little dragon blinks twice and then stares at me from his position on Eir's shoulder.

The dark elf directs another scowl at me, and her words become clipped with annoyance. "As you can see, he does blink. But what I'm trying to say, if you listen, is that that tongue clears it to work as a third eye."

"Ahh." Eir lifts a finger as though a light bulb of understanding is attached to it. "You mean like opening inner vision?" She tucks a loose strand of brown hair behind one ear. "I think I read about this in a book about peaceful magic."

"Yes, like I said." Slight relief spreads across the elf's face. "But it's not just for peaceful magic. It's used for all magic and giving an insight into other things."

Led by Elaith, we push farther through the trees, dodging low branches.

After a few moments, the dark elf rubs her chin. "I can tell Zildryss is correct. You need a lot more training. Come. We must begin before you go back to the light elves. As much as dark elves think they can get away with kidnapping you, I'm pretty sure Freya could track your movements and know your whereabouts. If you don't turn up back at your village on time, he will come searching."

Again, that niggling distrust squelches through my stomach. "How do you know so much?"

Elaith nods at the dragon. "Simple. He's shown me."

Attempting to keep my expression unreadable, I gaze at the dragon. "Oh."

Zildryss licks from one eye to the next, his eyes fixed on me. Suddenly, a vision of me riding Elan and plummeting safely from an immense height on her back fills my mind. I can almost feel the wind on my face even though I know I'm standing on the ground.

I tilt my face toward the sky. "I miss that feeling." I stare at Zildryss. "Did you do that?"

Remaining on Eir's shoulder with eyes fixed on me, he continues to lick one eye then the other.

Elaith studies me. "If you just had a clear vision and it's not a normal gift you possess, then Zildryss was the one who put it there. Come. We need to keep moving. We'll take you somewhere safer within the dark elves' area."

"Are there markings that distinguish between the dark and light elf areas?" I ask.

Elaith's eyebrows rise. "Yes. Didn't the light elves tell you?"

I shake my head.

"I didn't think they'd be that ignorant. They should've told you the areas the dark elves occupy. Maybe they just assumed you would be able to escape or avoid the dark elves. The ignorance!" She hisses and kicks at the dirt before pushing back some drooping tendrils of weeping willow branches thickly blocking our way.

We push through behind her, entering a small plain surrounded by trees with the same thick foliage.

"We should be safe here. The dragon suggested the spot."

I stare at the dragon, dumbfounded. He and the dark elf going against her kind seems quite unusual.

Eir lifts her hand toward the little dragon, and he crawls onto it, using it like a pedestal. "This dragon holds so many unusual gifts. Are there other dragons like it?"

"This dragon is rare. Others with such gifts are rarer, but they do exist."

Zildryss pushes off Eir's hand and flies to a branch above to stare down at us.

With eyes full of affection, Elaith follows the drag-on's movements. "The dragon's opted to keep watch. He does that sometimes." She paces a small area, her boots making light thuds in the soft dirt. Her eyes trail the treed edge of the plain while she sweeps back the dark strands of hair tainted with silver and weaves them into a braid before tying it off at the back of her neck. This exposes her face, illuminated by the light of day. Her skin is pale, as though she has spent too much time underground, and many of her features—the long, thin face; hollow cheekbones; and sharp, dark eyes; along with the pointy ears—are much the same as those of the dark elves that invaded Asgard. This is no surprise, though those elves seemed more serene and sinister. While she is distracted, I study her for anything that might reveal her to be Loki in another one of his shifting forms. He has tricked me too many times, and I'm suspicious of nearly every new person or being that acts slightly different from the rest. If she isn't Loki, I need to know the answer to one pressing question.

"I don't understand why you're helping us. Are you planning on leaving the dark elves?"

She shakes her head, firm and decisive. "I plan on staying with the dark elves." Her dark eyes land on me in a determined warning. "Make no mistake, I'm a dark elf through and through, but there are some things that I do against their wishes. Sometimes I follow the pull of my gut to do what I see fit."

I swallow—that almost sounds like a threat. However, since she's helping us, I decide that's just her personality and she must not be great with beings other than animals. "Oh. That seems rather risky, to do that to the race you want to stay with."

The intensity of her gaze softens, and she halts, splaying her feet and focusing on the ground. "Yes, it is. There've been many times the dark elves have questioned me. Thankfully, they have pardoned my devious ways as something I do because I'm more independent. Or because at different points in time, almost every one of them has done what they felt they needed to do, going against the group." She raises her gaze to the dragon, sitting in the branches above, and her anguish seems to fade. "We're here for our own gain and not so much as a group. We rarely work as a group against something." She lowers her eyes to us and squints. "Where are your weapons?"

The sudden mention reminds me of the emptiness at my back, making me feel awkward. "They're in the cabin. We thought we were in a safe area, and they look peculiar with the gowns."

Elaith shrugs. "In any case, I should have enough weapons here for you to work with."

Eir's brow wrinkles. "But aren't you teaching us magic, not combat skills?"

"Yes." The dark elf's short answer leaves Eir and me looking at each other in confusion.

Then the sound of sliding swords rings through

the air. I'm not even sure where they came from. By the time I find the source of the noise, I'm shocked to find arrows, spears, and swords floating in the air. Suddenly, all these sharp weapons turn and point toward us, flying as one in our direction.

I find myself again questioning if this dark elf is on our side or if she's trying to kill us herself.

Chapter Sixteen

Instinctively, I block the flying weapons with a wave of my hands, building a protective barrier. In my peripheral vision, Eir does the same. They crash into our barrier before clanging to the ground.

Elaith's eyebrows rise, and a satisfied smirk crosses her face. "Good. You have learned some defense magic." She circles the weapons on the ground, nudging them into a tight pile with a boot. "I assume that Gilroma taught you this."

I become suspicious as this comment captures my unwavering gaze. "How do you know Gilroma?"

Her smirk deepens, and her dark eyes seem to dance with glee as they connect with mine. "Gilroma is a friend of mine."

I squint, unable to hide my suspicion. "Don't you mean *Loki*?"

She shrugs. "Loki, Gilroma… it doesn't matter."

I catch Eir's gaze to see if she's thinking the same

as I am. She seems to be. I cross my arms and lean on one leg. "It does to me."

Elaith quirks an eyebrow as though she finds my reaction amusing. "Whatever form he wore, he always had your best interest in heart."

I scoff. "What are you? Another one of his mistresses?"

The dark elf's laugh sounds almost like a bell pealing, high pitched and joyous. "Highly unlikely. He's not my type."

"Which part? The lying and conniving Loki, or Gilroma the dark elf?"

"Whichever suits you best." With a wave of a hand, she gathers all the weapons and sends them outside our immediate training area. "Now, shall we get on with the lesson?"

I tighten the cross of my arms and rest them heavily against my stomach. "Fine. Let's get this over with."

DEEP GOLDEN HUES mixed with orange, red, and darkening blue fill the sky. The sunset is a sign that our lesson must end. The dark elf has taught us much dark magic and some light magic, often incorporating them together. I was surprised by how so many moves were a fine line between both forms. My head is exploding with new techniques and things to remember, and the time has passed quickly, making our lesson with Aymar seem slow.

A strong breeze blows through the weeping willows, their rustling leaves playing their chorus to the rhythm of the wind, drawing the attention of our teacher to the darkening sky.

"You should be heading back. Freyr may come looking for you if you're not back by mealtime."

The announcement brought a mixture of relief and sadness. Her lessons have taught us more and made me realize we have much more to learn.

"Will you teach us again?" I ask.

Zildryss pushes off the branch he was sitting on and circles lower, his lilac wings catching the glow of the setting sun and coating them with an orange tinge.

Elaith releases her hair, flicking her head to loosen the strands, her dark eyes following the little drag-on's moves. "Zildryss wants me to."

Unexpectantly, the little dragon circles one more time and lands on my shoulder, startling me. I don't know why, but I was expecting him to land on Elaith.

The dark elf catches my reaction. "The dragon wants to come with you. Zildryss has asked for me to continue your studies, and he will show you when to come."

A flash of lilac passes under my chin as he circles my neck, nestling against my skin at the back. "Will the light elves allow him into the village?"

A look of confusion covers the dark elf's face. "Why wouldn't they?"

I rub my upper arm, the leather of my uniform smooth under my fingers. "I thought because he's been living with the dark elves, he wouldn't be allowed in the light elves' village."

"The dragons are free to go where they choose. I don't think the light elves would hold anything against these dragons. Although their breed is rare, the long-mouthed guardians are revered and welcome almost everywhere. Besides, the light elves probably don't know he's been hanging around with me."

The dragon moves around my neck, pressing forward on my shoulder and staring up at me, his tongue flicking from one eye to the other.

I'm not sure if it's best I stare him in the eye, but pulling my gaze away is hard. "Is he seeing another vision?"

Elaith shrugs. "Maybe. He reveals to you what he wants when he wants." She ushers us off with a shooing action. "Now, off you go before they come looking for you. I don't need Freyr snooping around this area."

Eir stands beside me, her brow wrinkled. "But we don't know which way to go."

With a wave of a hand, all the weapons Elaith had conjured earlier disappear. "You have the dragon. He will lead you out of this area to the light elf village." As suddenly as she appeared, the dark elf disappears behind the branches of the weeping willows.

Brushing aside dangling willow branches, we head in the opposite direction. Our sense of direction was destroyed after escaping the underground by cutting through the mountain. We reach a field of flowers, and butterflies flutter away from us in all directions as we cut through. A pale-blue butterfly with light-brown markings floats briefly around my face. Zildryss springs to life and snaps his jaws over the butterfly, swallowing it body first with a couple of thrusts of the neck.

"Wow! That was quick!" Eir eyes the little dragon in awe.

We reach the other side of the floral plain, and I stare into the forest, not sure which way to go. Zildryss pushes off my shoulder and hovers a few yards in front of us. Slowly, he flies slightly to the left, now and then circling to see if we are following. As time goes on, the birds quiet their chirping as they settle in for the night. We follow Zildryss until the sun almost disappears, leaving dark, eerie shadows lurking under the trees. We hurry until a loud crashing noise breaks the silence, scaring us into statues.

I press up against a tree, and Zildryss lands on Eir's shoulder as she imitates me at the tree next to mine, her eyes wide as we search for the cause of the noise. Foliage cracks and rustles, growing louder and closer.

Something blue pushes through the gap in the trees, knocking branches and stepping loudly on twigs.

Eir moves away from the shelter of her tree. "Naga."

The blue dragon charges up to Eir, excitement radiating through every pore until his eyes land on Zildryss and widen. *How cute is this dragon? So tiny. Naga thought Naga was tiny, but this one is much smaller,* he says excitedly. His eyes fix on the little dragon, then he throws his head high as though he just remembered something. *Elan, I've found them!* he calls.

A thundering sounds through the forest until a golden dragon charges through the bushes, feet pummeling the ground.

Elan slides to a halt in front of me, her eyes

lowering to check every part of my body. *Oh, thank dragon scales! We thought we lost you. We've been looking for you everywhere.* She stands straight and towers overhead, studying my back. *Are you hurt?*

I chuckle, lightly shoving her, and she sits in front of me. "We're fine. We got slightly sidetracked. Aymar was missing from our lesson this morning, so we went to discover the realm. In the process, we kind of got kidnapped by dark elves."

What?

I cringe at Elan yelling in my mind and push my palms down in a calming motion. "Quiet down. It's all good. We were rescued by this little guy and a dark-magic teacher."

Elan twists her mouth, her eyes full of disappointment. *I can never leave you alone.*

I smile cheekily. "You didn't. You left me with Eir."

Her scales bunch together above her eyes in a frown. *You know what I mean.*

Attempting to change the subject, I ask, "Have you seen our magic teacher today?"

Zildryss flies to my shoulder and stares up at Elan.

I think I saw him in the food hall not long ago. She eyes the little dragon on my shoulder. *Where did you find this little guy?*

"He found us. Apparently, he's a long-mouthed guardian."

Her golden eyes fix on Zildryss, studying him intensely. *A long-mouthed guardian! They're extremely rare. I haven't even seen one before.*

The little dragon charges down my body and onto the ground to circle Elan several times at a speed I didn't think possible. He stops in front of her, folding a wing across his chest, and bows.

Eir holds a hand over her heart. "Aw. How cute. The little guy even knows that Elan is an Emperor dragon."

Elan's golden eyes soften, and she lowers her nose to the tiny dragon. Zildryss climbs on and peers into her eyes while licking his own, one then the other.

She chuckles as he climbs up her back, pulling on the scales lining her neck. *I like him. He's funny.* Suddenly, her neck stiffens, and she peers up as though attempting to look at him. *Ah. He just showed me something. That's an interesting way to communicate.*

"What did he show you?" I ask.

She grins. *He showed me that we could be great friends. All of us. Him included.*

Chapter Seventeen

Zildryss flies up to Eir's shoulder to circle his tail around the back of her neck. His dreamy eyes, full of admiration for the larger dragons, especially Elan, barely leave them.

I shake my head. "That's really cute. He seems to adore you two."

Eir giggles. "Doesn't he!"

Naga makes a strange noise that sounds slightly like a snort. *Well, Naga and Elan adore him.*

Following the dragons' lead, we reach the edge of the village by nightfall.

"I think we need to find Aymar even though it's late. We should see if everything is good for our lesson tomorrow."

Eir strokes the little dragon over the crown of his head and between his eyes. "You know me. I'm always happy to learn more light magic. However, can we make sure we arrange this for tomorrow? I'm exhausted."

"Me too. I just want to see that Aymar will be around tomorrow."

A frown creases Eir's forehead. "Tell me, though. How did you find the magic Elaith taught us? I found it a little strange that the dark magic wasn't that dark. When Gilroma taught us, it used to feel… I don't know… eerie at times. The way Elaith taught us today, maybe I'm not so against the magic after all."

I nod. "It did seem to be more balanced. Perhaps she was teaching us this way because of Zildryss. She seems to take his advice seriously. Maybe there isn't that much of a difference between light and dark magic. It could be it's just how it's executed." We pause outside the village, and I take the tip of Elan's jaw in my hand. "We shall catch up later."

She lowers her gaze at me, her eyes stern. *Yes. Especially if you plan on going for a walk around this realm by yourself.*

"Bu—"

Next time, take me. She cuts me off, scowling.

I tap her lightly on the nose and chuckle. "You're not my personal bodyguard, Elan. But if you're around, I shall certainly take you."

She huffs, covering me in warm breath. *Great.*

Now I have to wait around all day just to see if you want to go discovering without me.

"No. You don't. You are your own free dragon. And you know I can stand up for myself." As I turn to leave, a flash of lilac catches my eye. I follow it to find Zildryss on Elan's back, preparing to nestle into her shoulder.

"I guess the little guy doesn't want to come with us." Eir pouts, placing a lightheartedness on her disappointment.

The little dragon's tongue licks from one eye to the other, wearing a look similar to a smirk.

I shrug. "It doesn't matter. I think he'll be back soon. He can get to know Elan and Naga a bit more. If he plans on staying with us, then he also needs to get to know the dragons."

Naga will look after him. Naga's happy to find a new friend. The blue dragon's big eyes barely leave the little dragon sitting on Elan's shoulder, the little dragon returning his gaze with almost as much affection.

I smile and call over my shoulder, "Okay. See you guys later."

We arrive at the area where we trained with Aymar to find him with his feet up on a green reclining chair, which he must have conjured, and his hands behind his head. With his eyes closed, his face is peaceful, and his belt hangs undone at his sides as though he recently finished an eating fest.

I clear my throat as we enter the area under the drooping vine ceiling.

His eyes open, widening upon observing our clothes. "What are you wearing?"

I swallow. I'd forgotten about our changing into tight-fitting leather, the kind of clothes I'm accustomed to.

He rises to his feet, letting his belt dangle loosely from its loops by his sides, circling us. "You're dressed like the dark elves. Where are your beautiful pale gowns that the light elves gave you?"

Brushing my hands over the leather, I revel in its familiar texture. "This is a disguise. We had to escape from the dark elves."

He pauses in front of us, his face pale. "How did you get caught?"

"We were bored when you weren't here this morning, so we went for a walk." Eir eyes him with suspicion. "Where were you, anyway?"

Ignoring her question, Aymar asks, "Did you use light magic to escape?"

I shake my head. "No. A dark elf assisted us."

A deep frown creases the smooth skin of his forehead as he turns away. A moment later, he faces us again, and his expression flattens as though everything is normal and the conversation never happened. He claps his hands and rubs them together. "Okay. When would you like to start your next lesson?"

A surprising amount of annoyance shows on Eir's face as she crosses her arms. "We were here before to take our lesson, but you weren't." She repeats the question he ignored. "Where were you? We thought we had a lesson with you every day."

The light elf chuckles, busying himself by grabbing his belt and attempting to do it up. "Well, you're here now, aren't you?" He yanks harder at the strap, and the clasp finally reaches. "It's a new day."

I scowl. "Do you class the end of the day as a new day even when the sun has gone down?"

The light elf shakes a forefinger at us. "Now, now. There is no need for that just because I like to sleep in."

Holding back a groan, I give up on the questioning and make eye contact with Eir. Though I'm exhausted from training with Elaith, something tells me we should keep that secret from this elf. Dark rings circle Eir's eyes in the dim light of a glowing rock on a post. Even though she looks more tired than I feel, she nods, a glint of caution in her eye. From what we were told, all dark elves are evil, yet one helped us... though she might have been Loki in disguise. On the other hand, light elves are supposed to be open and honest, and this one is avoiding our questions for some strange reason.

My shoulders cave as I will some of the exhaustion to leach away. "Okay, let's start our lesson, then." I hold up a finger. "As long as we're not conjuring up more food."

Aymar chuckles. "Don't worry. I've had more than enough food today." He rubs his potbelly as his eyes drop to our clothes. "First, though, you need to get out of those horrid leathers. I don't know why you would wear them when you don't have to. That can be your first magic trick for the day."

I feel like telling him that is not even close to our first magic wielded for today, but I leave it, and with a wave of a hand, I change both my and Eir's leather clothes into the gowns the light elves wear.

"Perfect. Now I can concentrate. Okay then, let's start by creating plants that have healing properties."

My mouth drops open. "You can do that?"

His belly shakes as he chuckles again. "Of course. It's light magic. Usually, magic means you can do almost anything." He spreads his arms wide, his sleeves drooping as he pulls his eyes from Eir to me. "Now, picture a healing plant. I'm sure Anita has shown you a few."

My eyebrows crumple together. "How do you know about Anita?"

A nervousness fills his eyes as he chuckles. "My dear, I know a great deal more than what I let on. And Anita is a powerful healer in Asgard… in case you didn't already know."

Placing a hand on my hip, I rock onto one leg. "Of course I know. That's why she's the main healer they use when they have a big battle on Asgard. She worked hard to gain a reputation and change her path as a wingless Valkyrie before I come along. She was a fantastic support when I worked on changing Odin's ways and eventually opening his eyes to seeing that wingless Valkyries should be able to reap souls for Valhalla also. And someone with the dedication Anita has shown is going to be a powerful person."

He taps my elbow lightly. "No need to gloat. I know about your history." He winks to add some humor, but that only manages to stir the pot simmering in my stomach. "Okay, then. You need to picture the individual leaves then the stem of the plant, just like you did with the food."

I work tirelessly on this task, focusing on the individual leaves emerging out of the ground, only to have them disappear on me when exhaustion takes over and I lose the train of thought. Eventually, I manage to draw the leaves out of the ground, followed by the stem, coaxing it to grow until it produces a flower useful for medicinal purposes.

"I did it!" I cry, tears gathering in the corners of my eyes as I gaze down at the beautiful, healthy plant.

Aymar stoops, picks the flower, and sniffs it, which irritates me and instantly dries my eyes, especially when he pulls it apart and munches on the petals.

A strange glaze covers his eyes moments after he swallows. "Phew! Well, I don't need to eat much of that flower to know you've succeeded in creating the right one." He puffs out a breath and wobbles slightly, placing the remaining flower on the ground next to the plant. "It definitely has a sedative effect. I may become a completely different teacher if I consume any more." He observes Eir's creation of an almost identical plant, scoops up a petal, and throws it into his mouth. His eyes glaze over, and he chuckles as he stumbles to his green chair. "Okay. I've definitely had my quota for the day." Slumping back on the chair, he stretches his legs out into the position he was in when we arrived. His broad smile is giddy, and he crosses his legs at the ankles. Sighing audibly, he laces his hands behind his head, his words slurring. "You two have come a long way in just a short period. I have much hope for you yet."

Eir arches an eyebrow. "And what are we going to learn next?"

Aymar works his mouth, clicking his tongue against its roof.

When he doesn't answer, Eir continues in annoyance, "I feel like we have much more to learn today. We want to increase our magic, and Kara needs to use her time here wisely before she's allowed to return to Asgard."

Our instructor yawns loudly, eventually covering his mouth with a hand as though it's a second thought. "Of course, of course. Let me think." He touches a finger to his temple a few times and raises his finger. "Aha. I've got it. I want you to bring up a visualization of your love interest."

"What?" I snap.

Chapter Eighteen

The light elf waves a hand at me, his face slackening further as he fails to enunciate. "Suuurely you have some kind of looove interest. Valkyries asss preeetty as you twooo wooould have sooomebooody of innnterest one waaay or anooother."

Eir shakes a finger at our teacher, who is clearly wiped out by the sedative. "Have you been talking to Naga?"

"Light elvesss aaare friends ooof Nagaaa." Slowly he frowns. "Naga? Who's Nagaaa?" He holds up a finger. "Ah. Nagaaa. The cuuute laaarge, yeeet smmmall bluuue draaagon." He shakes his head to clear it. "Yes, Naga is a veeery clevvver boooy." He holds out his hand, and a glass of liquid appears within his grasp. Aymar drinks it until the contents are gone. "Ah. That's better." His words are suddenly clearer. He puffs out a loud breath. "Wow! Those petals were strong. Good job!" He places the glass on the ground next to his chair and sits straighter. "Now, where were we?" He slaps his thigh lightly. "That's right. Naga cares about his Valkyrie. He wants his Valkyrie to find a good mate."

"Seriously?" I ask in disbelief.

He focuses on me. "Your dragon hasn't said much, but I'm sure she wishes you to be mated off too."

I wipe my hands down the sides of my face, and Aymar's chuckle stops my protest before I can start. "In any case, this exercise is all in the good practice of magic." His words still come out slow as an aftereffect of the sedative plant yet much clearer than before. "You should conjure up an image of your love interest."

Hiding my displeasure out of respect for my teacher is impossible. "But why a love interest?" I flail my arms to my sides. "Why can't I conjure up anybody I have an interest in, like a friend?"

"Because a love interest drums up a stronger feeling than a person you like as a friend, and it's easier to work with the emotion." He shrugs. "Besides, you're more likely to have their image embedded in your mind. You would have studied and memorized every single aspect of their face and body that you could see."

"What if you don't have one?" Smugly, I raise my chin.

Again, he chuckles, which is starting to get on my nerves. "Everybody has some kind of interest or attraction to somebody. Even if it isn't love. I'm sure even someone as battle friendly as you has one." With a casual wave of a hand, he focuses on Eir. "Let the peaceful one go first. She probably has someone even if she's not ready to settle down."

Eir runs her fingers through a long strand of brown hair fallen from her plait, a nervous gesture as she glances at the light elf. "All right. I shall give it a go. Do I have to build this person in my mind first? Or do I just let it grow from my subconscious and allow it to bring up whomever?"

"In this case, let your subconscious bring the person of interest forward." His speech pattern quickens to his normal speech pace, sounding more coherent. "Remember, take a deep breath in and release it slowly. You want peace to overcome your body. It's the only way to pull the true person out."

Eir closes her eyes and clasps her hands to steer her consciousness. Then she focuses on a spot before her as her chest expands within her gown, from a deep breath.

Her long brown eyelashes fold over her pale-skinned cheeks as her eyes close and creases of concentration line her face. After she takes a few more deep breaths, an image starts to appear. I'm unprepared for what I see—a clear-cut hologram of a tall elf with pale, freckled skin and auburn hair flowing past his shoulders. His square jawline is masculine yet softened by the peace shining in his green eyes, which would certainly match Eir's personality. He isn't what I would call stunning, instead ordinary with a couple of handsome features.

My mouth drops in shock. This elf is wearing the tunic of the light elves from the village. I haven't seen him, but Eir clearly has. When the edges of his hologram sharpen, Eir opens her eyes, and a pleased smile spreads across her face.

Pointing at the image, I ask, "Who's that?"

Redness fills Eir's cheeks, her eyes filled with admiration as she gazes at him. "He's one of the light elves in the village. I met him when you were sleeping on the day we arrived. He's rather sweet, and he gave off a peaceful vibe."

I nod. "Okay. That was quick. He does have a friendly face." For Eir's sake, I'm trying to be diplomatic and keep an open mind. A light elf is probably a good match for her. She is one of a kind, being a peaceful Valkyrie. We're supposed to be battle maidens.

Aymar claps and nods in approval. "Excellent."

Rising from his chair, the light-magic teacher circles the hologram as his eyebrows rise into golden-blond peaks. "Yes, yes. He's actually a lovely person. You would probably like him immensely if you got to know him." A sly smile lights his face. "It may make Naga one happy dragon."

His focus lands on me, and he raises his chin expectantly. "Now, it's your turn."

I cringe. "I told you. I don't have a love interest," I protest, not wanting to partake in this exercise.

He places a hand on my forearm. "You'd be surprised. You don't know until you try." His eyes bore into my soul. "Your heart may long for someone that you are refusing to accept. This is also a part of that magic lesson—opening your heart." He circles one hand in a motion to hurry. "I insist you do it."

My arms droop by my sides. "But how is this going to help us in any dilemma?"

"You may be stuck in a situation where you are in desperate need of a reminder of people who care about you. Maybe visualizing a person you care about deeply will spur you on to tackle your obstacle, to protect them, or to help you pursue the final task needed."

I groan. "All right," I say with a hint of annoyance. Following Eir's movements, I close my eyes, cupping my hands together in front of my chest in an almost prayerlike fashion. I let a deep breath fill my lungs, flooding them with oxygen to aid the tension in leaving every muscle of my body. Despite my determination that I don't have a love interest, any magical exercise bestowed upon me could benefit me. I must learn all kinds of magic as quickly as possible.

Magic fires through me, pushing forward even though I don't believe I have anybody to conjure. I can feel the magic growing, forming something in front of me. No image appears in my mind, and my mind remains closed, allowing my subconscious to take over and project whatever Aymar believes is tucked deep inside of me, so deep that I'm not aware of it. Soon, I feel the process ending, and I move my hands in a circle to complete the final task.

To my left, Eir gasps and sounds as though she slaps a hand over her mouth.

The sound draws my eyes open, and the image in front of me floods me with disbelief.

"No." I blink, trying to will the image away and unconsciously retreating, my heart screaming protests. "This can't be right." I glare at the magic teacher. "What sort of a sick joke is this?"

His eyes dance with pleasure and amusement as he observes the figure in front of me. As my eyes narrow on the figure, he says, "It's coming from your subconscious. There's no sick magic. It's your inner self expressing who is loved by your heart."

I gape at the figure in front of me, cloaked in black leather and framed by large black wings. Dark-brown eyebrows arch over the blackest of eyes, which have melted my heart in the past and shown me kindness. They are handsome features that will haunt me in my dreams. Registering the angel of death standing in front of me drags up a loathing like no other as I relive a deep sense of betrayal and guilt. I push aside my hurt and disbelief as I glare at the form of Harut.

Chapter Nineteen

"This has got to be a joke." I throw my arms toward the image in front of me and glare at the projection of Harut, my supposed love interest.

Aymar chuckles, rising to his feet and backing up a step. "This is of your conjuring, not mine." Amusement dances in his eyes, yet something I can't read lies in them also. It seems like sadness. "No, it isn't my doing," he repeats. "It's purely from you."

Stamping a foot, I ball my hands into fists. "But he betrayed me! He..." I stammer, my tongue refusing to work while bathed in shock. "He..." Every muscle in my arms tenses as my fists tighten. "He betrayed me at the most inconvenient time. And he betrayed me when he was supposed to be working with me to protect Asgard. Instead, he turned around and betrayed Asgard under the disguise of many forms." I groan. "That is the one thing that I despise the most. I thought I had two powerful friends by my side to protect Asgard. Instead, he changed. Both of my powerful friends were Loki in disguise, and he rode a dragon army against us." I throw my hands again at the projection of Harut, my voice rising to almost a yell. "He's not even a real person."

The strange expression remains in Aymar's eyes as he shrugs. "Maybe that's all your heart can accept right now—someone who isn't real, someone you've built up in your mind that isn't who you think they are. Or to protect your heart, deep down, you've built up a new thought, convincing yourself he wasn't that person who deceived you."

Swiping my hands at Aymar, I scream, "Stop this! This is such a farce!"

Eir braces my shoulders with her hands, and I pull my glaring eyes from Harut to Aymar, my turmoil deepening when I can't read the strange expression on his chubby face.

Eir squeezes my shoulders, her peaceful aura attempting to assuage my tumult. "It's okay, Kara." Her voice is soft and calming, trying to flatten the waves roiling inside me. "In my opinion, he's gone." She swipes a hand at the image, and it disappears.

My glare returns to the magic teacher. "I will

never need to use that magic." My words force their way through my clenched teeth. "That's ridiculous. Clearly, it doesn't do anything useful."

Gazing at Eir, Aymar spreads his arms wide, back to his usual jolly self, seemingly without a care in the world. "What's up with her?"

Eir blocks his view of me, her body ridged with a warning. "Stop, Aymar! That's enough."

I blink in surprise at the harshness of the peaceful Valkyrie's words.

Feigning hurt, he places a finger over his lips in a shushing motion, sealing his lips tightly. Yet his eyes dance with amusement as he sits back down on his chair.

His actions are strange and incomprehensible, and I feel he is making fun of me. Anger roils in my stomach, and out of spite, I imagine myself in my fighting leathers. The costume changes right in front of him. A satisfied sneer rises to my face when his eyes widen with understanding, taking in my uniform and act of defiance.

My anger churns dangerously, unlike anything I've felt before, and I realize I have to take action before I do something I'll regret. "I'm done with magic for today." I storm out of the vine-covered area. "Are you coming, Eir?"

Hurried footsteps follow me, barely heard over Aymar's voice calling after us.

"Make sure you're here tomorrow. You're required to practice every day until you leave this village. I promised that to Freyr."

My annoyance burns so deep within my gut that not turning around to punch the little weasel in the face takes all my effort.

When we manage to leave his earshot, I grumble, "That was a nasty trick he played on me."

Eir quickens her footsteps and matches my stride, wrapping an arm around my shoulders. She speaks hesitantly. "I know you think it was a trick, but I don't think it was."

My shoulders stiffen, ready to shake off Eir's embrace.

"That's okay," she says in a rush. "I'm not saying this as a judgment. You have many mixed emotions about what happened and what Loki did to you. They are completely understandable. I can't wait to catch that weasel and lock him up again." She squeezes my shoulders until some tension seeps away. "And I'm going to help you every step of the way."

Tilting my head, I rest it on her shoulder. "Thanks, Eir. I appreciate you coming here with me —you and Naga."

We approach our little cottage, and a lilac streak flashes through the air and lands on my shoulder before circling my neck and nudging against me.

"Hey, little guy."

The scales, softer than Elan's and more like a snake's, rub against my skin. He tilts his head up, letting me rub him under the chin.

"I'm happy to see you."

Elan stomps around the corner of the cottage, her head leveling with mine. *What about me?*

I rub under a scale at the side of her face, feeling the roughness with my hand. "I'm always happy to see you, Elan."

Her large golden-brown eyes focus on me. *You look down. You should be happy after a magic lesson.*

Sidestepping her, I stomp toward the cottage. "I don't want to talk about it." Stopping at the door with Zildryss still curled around my neck, I turn to see if Eir is following.

Eir runs a hand up her snout. "Don't worry, Elan. She's a little upset because we had to pull up a person of interest."

The scales between her eyes bunch together in a frown. *What do you mean?*

"A love interest," Eir explains.

Naga darts toward Eir, excitement on his

face. *Does Eir have a love interest?* His big blue eyes scan Eir's demeanor. *That would make Naga happy.*

Eir giggles as her eyes shine with happiness. "Yes, I know it would. You'll be happy to know I did pull up someone."

Naga's front talons dance alternatively. *Naga can't wait to meet him.*

"Naga will have to wait." Eir reaches for Naga's nose. "I haven't had much to do with him, but he's an interest."

Is he peaceful?

She runs a hand down the bridge of his nose, her fingers tracing the edges of a couple of scales. "Of course he's peaceful, Naga."

Elan interrupts, her eyes showing a keenness I'd prefer was absent. *And what about Kara?*

Eir's voice lowers. "Kara pulled up Harut."

Elan's voice remains in my head as I decide I've heard enough and slam the cottage door behind me then throw myself stomach first onto my bed, Zildryss taking flight before I land.

Oh, I understand why she's upset, then. We'll give you two some peace.

The door groans open, and Eir calls back, "Thanks, Elan. See you soon."

The hinges squeak, and the door clicks shut. Soft footsteps approach on the wooden boards. The mattress tips as Eir sits on the edge and rubs my shoulder blades with her palm.

Zildryss's scales rub against my arm, bringing warmth as he curls against my pillow.

Eir presses deeper, making pressure points scream in my back. "It's okay, Kara. Forget about what you saw. Maybe it is some sort of magic trick. I'm not sure. But it's not worth worrying about it. Just because he formed in front of you doesn't mean he's your love interest."

Rolling to the side to look at her, I almost crush the little dragon. He quickly scurries to the other side of the pillow, his lilac pupils staring at me.

I stroke the top of his head, and his face relaxes as he leans into my touch. "Then why did Aymar say the image came from my subconscious? It's not fair. I don't want to think of Harut at all. He wasn't even real."

The peaceful Valkyrie looks sheepish, yet understanding also shines in her eyes. "Maybe because it was kind of your first love."

My eyes narrow despite the thoughtfulness of her tone.

Holding up her hands in defense, she says, "Not that anything happened between you two, but he was one of the first people who stood up for you other than the wingless Valkyries. It was sweet of him to help you. It just ruined it all when you found out who he really was. And I completely get that." She threads a lock of my long brunette hair behind my ear. "You have every right to be upset."

The little dragon patters up to my face and licks my cheek. His tongue is coarse, and I flinch before chuckling with surprise.

Using the back of my hand, I wipe my cheek, feeling more lighthearted. "What was that for?"

Zildryss blinks and licks one eye then the other before charging at me and licking me again with his long tongue, designed to catch insects. My spirits lighten, and I sit up. The tiny dragon crawls onto my lap and stares into my eyes.

I run a finger over the top of his head, following the rise and fall of his spikes down his spine and being careful to miss the sharp points. "This is one cute dragon. I have no idea why he's decided to come with us, but I appreciate it."

Zildryss seems to smile at me. At the same time, a comical image of Harut projects into my thoughts. Then a paintbrush strokes across his image, wiping away his existence more with each swipe until he is gone. A strange joy rises from within me, and I can't help smiling.

Lifting the little dragon onto my palm, I raise him

toward my head. "You know exactly what my heart feels. Thank you."

Zildryss sits on his haunches and scratches behind one eye as though nothing unusual just took place.

Chapter Twenty

The next morning, I wake to find the little dragon cuddled next to my pillow. After a second, he opens one eye and sleepily gazes at me for a few moments before opening the other slightly. Pushing up into a sitting position, I find Eir's bed empty, and she's not in the cottage.

Zildryss stretches his front legs beside me before tilting all his weight onto them and kicking his back legs out.

"Do you know where Eir went?" I ask the little dragon, not expecting an answer.

His long tongue licks from one eye to the other, and he blinks. An image of Eir walking through the village enters my mind, and with her is the love interest she conjured yesterday. She giggles and loops her arm through his before the image disappears.

Dumbfounded at the sudden vision, I stare at the little dragon. "Did you do that?"

Looking innocent, Zildryss nods once.

"Then I must say you have an extraordinary gift there. Even though you don't speak, it's a rather efficient way of communicating."

Zildryss's wings tickle me as he circles on the spot then curls up against my body. After scooping him up in my hands, I rest him on my lap, his curious eyes never leaving my face. "Didn't you want to go with Eir?"

He shakes his head, a determined look on his tiny face.

"I guess you're right. Love interests need to be alone to see if it falls into place."

Not feeling like communicating with light elves this morning, I conjure my own food and eat it quite happily in the room, sharing pieces of fruit with the tiny dragon. I hold out a grape, and he snavels it up, crushing it in his mouth before swallowing it whole. The quiet breakfast with Zildryss seems to be the kind of company I need this morning, and my spirits rise slowly after yesterday's ordeal with Aymar.

Between mouthfuls, I ask Zildryss, "Should we go and learn from our light magic teacher this morning?"

The little dragon shakes his head, and an image of Elaith pops into my mind.

"So you think I should go to the dark elf to learn her magic first?"

Zildryss nods, and I give him another grape, watching with fascination as he crushes it and swallows it whole. The cabin door swings open with a slight squeak, and Eir stands within its frame.

I nudge the little dragon and tilt my head toward the door. "Ah, she's back from romanticizing."

A deep flush taints Eir's cheeks, and her mouth drops open. "How did you kn—" She gapes at Zildryss swallowing another grape. "Oh. Did you rat on me?"

Zildryss's mouth tilts up at the sides.

Eir scowls at him playfully then shrugs. "That's not fair." The color in her cheeks deepens. "I had to see if he is a good match."

I arch an eyebrow. "And?"

She gazes out the window and says hesitantly, "Yantolos is a peaceful village. I guess you could say that things are looking positive."

Waiting for her to continue, I feed Zildryss another grape.

She holds up a finger and says with more urgency, "But I have to give it time."

I shrug. "Take all the time you want. It's not like you've got a short life. And being a light elf, neither does he. They're almost immortal, aren't they?"

She clasps her hands in front of herself. "Not immortal. But they do have a long life, kind of like us."

"Have you had breakfast?" I lift my platter of food. "I still have plenty of food."

"I had a little, but that looks delicious." She grabs a blueberry pancake and takes a small bite. "What's the plan for today?"

A stroke the little dragon on the head, and he darts to the platter to grab another grape. "This little guy says we should go have another lesson with Elaith first, then maybe we should go to Aymar after."

Eir shrugs. "Sounds like a plan." She takes another mouthful of blueberry pancake and groans. "Oh, Kara. You conjure up the most delicious blueberry pancakes I've ever tasted."

"See, I can cook." I smirk.

Eir chuckles, slapping a hand over her mouth to stop it from spluttering.

"Hey!" I feign hurt. "That's not nice." And I laugh with her. "Thank goodness for magic, hey?"

She nods and clears her throat. Quickly, she finishes her pancake then gets dressed in the leather outfit I conjured yesterday.

After changing, I grab my bow, quiver, and sword and head toward the area where Elaith trained us yesterday. After not wearing weapons for a couple of days, carrying them on my back again feels strange. Since our last visit was a little more dangerous than what we'd experienced in this realm, we decide not to risk it. Not wanting to be questioned by the light elves over our outfits, weapons, and destination, we bypass the village and pass through the forest instead.

My fingers twitch by my sides when we reach the area where the dark elves captured us. I don't want a rerun of yesterday. Keeping our eyes peeled, we pass through the forest and stand at the lake's edge. A school of fish swim swiftly through the shallow water, making the area seem undisturbed.

An eerie feeling tickles the back of my neck. I spin around to find dark elves surrounding us in the same place again. *I can't believe it!* Zildryss circles my neck, his tail draping over my shoulder.

The main elf stalks forward. "I see you escaped, but not for long. I can't believe that you're stupid enough to come back into this area." He shrugs. "No matter. It gives us a chance to take you back where you belong."

Zildryss jumps off my shoulders and flies to the ground, landing a few feet in front of the dark elves. I frown, not knowing his intentions. Irritation flashes in the dark elf's eyes.

I extend my arm as though to stop the elf. "Don't hurt him."

The dark elf glowers then fixes his eyes on the little lilac dragon. "He's a dragon belonging to a dark elf. Why would I hurt him?"

Suddenly, Zildryss flicks his tail over his own head like a scorpion, and the point jabs straight into the ground in front of himself. The ground swallows each dark elf around us—the last elf reaching upward—and seals as though they were never there.

Eir gasps. "What just happened?"

As though feeling her distress, Zildryss flies to her shoulder, rubbing his cheek against her face. An image flashes into my mind, showing the dark elves landing safely within their cave below, in the room with the waterfall.

A look of satisfaction replaces Eir's distress. She turns to the little dragon and runs a hand down his ribs. "You're a tricky little boy when you want to be. You'll have to teach us how to do that."

An image of Elaith teaching us the magic flashes into my head.

I cross my arms and raise an eyebrow at the little dragon. "Okay, then. Where can we find Elaith?"

Another image of the dark elf standing in the spot we trained yesterday flashes inside my head. We weave our way through the forest until we spot the circle of weeping willows, their drooping branches concealing the clearing on the other side. The branches part as we pass through.

Elaith taps a boot against the grass. "So you finally arrived."

"We had a little trouble with some dark elves," I say.

"I assume the dragon took care of it."

"Yes. He did, and he said you would teach us how he did it."

Her foot stills. "What did he do?"

Eir lifts Zildryss off her shoulder, letting him rest on her hand. "He opened the ground and made them disappear straight through the earth and into their cave below."

"Ah, yes. I can teach you the basics. But you won't be as talented as this little guy. He has some serious talent for moving earth, just like he did when I rescued you yesterday."

I frown. "I thought that was you moving the earth."

She chuckles. "Oh, no. Only part of it. Most of it was him. Didn't you notice he was sitting on my shoulder when I needed to do the most significant moving?"

Zildryss flies off Eir's hand and into the trees.

Her wonder-filled eyes follow him. "Come to

think of it, I did notice, but I thought he was just being friendly."

Elaith gathers her silver-streaked hair back into a ponytail. "That, too, but it was mostly him. He has to be touching your skin to pass his magic through you." She releases an elastic band, which holds her hair, with a ping. "Right! Let's get straight to it." She splays her feet. "I need you to picture the ground opening up and a rock falling straight into it." The dark elf looks around. "You can practice on this rock by burying it in the ground."

To me, the rock was more like a boulder. "How do you expect us to be able to do that?"

"I believe it is much like your light elf would have taught you. You must picture it first then execute it from deep within yourself. Picture the earth moving sideways, breaking apart until it's big enough to devour the rock."

Doing this takes me several goes. First, I manage to sink only the bottom of my boulder in the earth with the majority sitting above.

Eir has a go at burying her boulder and manages to drop it halfway.

I close my eyes, determined to accomplish this before Eir does. Her light magic skills are quite something to behold. The thought of this alone makes focusing harder. I close off my ears to any distractions and imagine the earth separating, swallowing the boulder, and dusting the top with dirt. Within a few seconds, the ground rumbles under my feet, and I open my eyes just in time to see the boulder completely disappear into the ground, dust billowing in its wake.

A split second later, Eir's does the same.

"Excellent." Elaith clasps her hands behind her back. "Next, you will be doing it to each other. The first one to bury the other is the winner."

Chapter Twenty-One

Eir's face turns as pale as a ghost. "I can't do that! We'll kill each other."

A crooked smile doesn't reach the elf's eyes. "Trust me." She flicks at the tails on her long leather jacket. "I'll make sure you won't kill each other."

A shiver runs down my spine, and I can almost feel the dirt caking on my skin, burying me alive. Looking at the little dragon for answers, I pick up nothing. He scratches the side of his face with a back talon, looking casual and undeterred, as though this is all perfectly normal.

Eir holds my gaze. Her nervousness is a mirror of mine. Of course, we trust each other— we don't trust our inexperience and Elaith to rescue us if we fail. After a moment's pause, Eir nods once, indicating to go ahead.

All the strength seeps from my body, and I gape at the elf. "Are you kidding me?"

Unmoved, she shakes her head.

Shaking my arms and legs, I attempt to circulate my blood and retrieve my strength. "All right. Then you better protect the person that falls into the dirt. If you don't, there's going to be one angry Thor searching for you."

The dark elf shrugs. "If you say so. Then again, how's he going to know if you're buried?"

Using my magic, I lift the arrows out of my quiver, the weight on my back instantly lighter, and the points aim at the elf.

She holds up her hands in defense and snaps, "All right! I was trying to joke with you. It doesn't come easily to a dark elf. Obviously, I failed."

Still hesitant, I return the arrows.

Elaith straightens her shoulders. "I promise I'll look after you. The trick is to make the hole just big enough to bury your subject up to the neck. If it's too big, they'll be buried alive."

I off-load my weapons a few feet away and take a deep breath to settle my emotions.

Setting my eyes on Eir, I wait until she places her weapons aside and focuses on me. Our eyes connect, and I sum her up, assessing her height and how deep to make the hole. Then I focus on the ground below Eir's feet, readying to open the earth.

The ground opens underneath me and swallows

me, stripping my focus away. Dirt brushes against my skin, higher and higher, and my panic rises with it. I struggle, wanting to break free from the ground surrounding my body. Instead, it encases my feet, legs, and hips then crawls up my torso, securing my arms by my sides until it covers my shoulders. Quickly, I suck in a breath when the dirt tickles my neck, and I brace myself, knowing I'm probably about to be sucked under. The soil squashes me on all sides, making breathing harder.

I'm petrified until the realization sinks in that I've stopped dropping. The dirt remains at the height of my neck. After taming my emotions, I gaze upward to congratulate Eir. She perfected the move in one go. Except, she's completely gone—only a few strands of long dark-brown hair trail from the grass.

I scream, "No!" Glancing out of the corner of my eye, I yell at Elaith, "Quick! Get her!" My hysteria rises. I've buried Eir. I've buried one of my most loyal friends. Yet I'm stuck deep within the ground, unable to dig her out. Again, I scream at the dark elf, who seems to be taking her time. "Hurry up! She can't breathe under there!" My voice is so high-pitched that I don't recognize it. My throat clamps with panic.

Moving too casually for my liking, Elaith raises a hand to stop me from yelling. I'm confident that, if I weren't buried, I would have bitten her. Slowly, she walks over to where the few strands of Eir's hair spout from the ground.

"Hurry up!" I scream at her, struggling within the confinement of the dirt. "She can't breathe! Remember you promised you'd look after us if we did this!"

The little dragon dives off his branch and circles Elaith before landing on the ground not far from Eir's hair. He waddles a wide circle around Eir's hair, stops, then flicks his tail over his head and jabs it into the ground again, using that scorpion move.

Elaith stands back as the ground opens and slowly pushes Eir to the surface. Her cheeks are flushed as she spits dirt from her mouth and sucks in a deep breath.

Tossing my head backward, I cry, "Oh, thank Vanir!" My heart slowly returns to an average pace as I gaze at the dragon with unprecedented powers strutting around as though he didn't do anything. "You're such a good little dragon." As Eir regains her color, I swear I haven't seen anything as beautiful as her in my entire life. "I'm sorry, Eir!"

Placing a hand over her heart, she says, "You gave me a bit of a scare." She chuckles slightly. "But it's all okay. You have to practice." Her face flattens as she realizes I'm still buried.

The ground shakes underneath me, and I suck in another breath, expecting to drop farther into its confinement. Instead, each particle of dirt falls away, giving me more freedom as I rise out of the ground.

The second my feet are free, I race forward and throw my arms around my peaceful friend. "I'm extremely sorry," I say again, my voice rough from all my screaming.

Returning my embrace, she strokes the back of my ponytail. "You need to settle down. As I said, I'm fine, and you need to practice."

Elaith stands a few feet away. "Exactly! As she says, you need to practice." She claps her hands together. "Come on."

"Now?" Disgusted by her lack of empathy, I drop my embrace. "She needs to catch her breath."

Eir squeezes my forearm. "I'm fine, Kara. Come, let's practice."

We practice about ten more times, my heart pumping profusely in my chest each time as I fear I'll bury Eir again. Even though the dragon rescued her, I hate the thought of her being trapped. Now when I mess up, Elaith moves more quickly, spinning her hands and working hard to retrieve Eir from any time under the ground. One time, Eir buries me too deep, confronting me with the nightmare I gave her. Being trapped under the dirt is dreadful.

Overall, Eir's attempts are much better than mine.

"You're a natural, Eir," I say.

She shakes her head. "No, I'm not. I've just practiced magic more than you over the last couple of years."

Elaith gets us to work on a couple of other things, pausing us soon afterward. "It's time for you to leave before you become corrupted. You need to practice some light magic."

My hands halt midswirl. "What do you mean *corrupted*?"

"Practicing dark magic all the time can corrupt you and can make it harder, sometimes impossible, to create light magic. It's another reason the dark elves are unusually dark and their hearts rotten."

I gape at her. "But yours doesn't seem rotten."

Her dark eyes turn intense. "It's on the verge. It's only survived so far because of this little dragon here." Her eyes soften when he flies down to her hand from a nearby branch. "Keep him close. He's a precious little thing."

Eir casts a worried glance at me before she asks Elaith, "Shouldn't you keep him if you're about to be corrupted? If he's the only thing keeping you from turning, it will make more sense if he stays with you."

Elaith shakes her head. "He has shown me that

this is the end of my path with him. I must try to do the rest on my own. He has insisted that you are his current responsibility." She tosses a hand our way as though shooing us to leave. "Now, go practice your light magic. Even if you're too weary, you must practice it."

The thought of what Aymar did to me yesterday still churns the anger in my gut. I scowl. "I don't want to go."

Elaith straightens her back and raises her chin. "You must."

Chapter Twenty-Two

The lesson with Elaith was interesting. I'm leaving feeling more empowered in dark magic. I improved enough to bury Eir to her neck most of the time. I was keen to learn more, but the dark elf made it clear she had finished training us today, with no mention of the future. I don't quite believe the notion of having to practice light magic to uphold the correct magical balance. Still, I'm not going to risk it at this stage. Besides, I need all the training I can get.

We make our way around the village, dump our weapons in our cabin, and change into our light elf gowns, remembering the face Aymar gave us yesterday.

The door squeaks as I swing it open and head outside. "I guess the dragons are gone for another discovery again."

Eir steps through the door with Zildryss draped

over one shoulder, contrasting with her long pale-blue gown. "Let them. They don't need to stand by our sides all the time. They need to be free."

"You don't need to tell me. I'm happy Naga and Elan are spending time together."

Zildryss flies from Eir's shoulder to mine and circles my neck.

"Are you coming with us, little guy?"

He settles against my neck.

"I take that as a yes." I stroke his nose. "It's always nice to have your company."

We trek through the forest to the usual spot. Once again, we find Aymar with his eyes closed, stretched out lazily on his chair. His legs are kicked up and crossed at the ankles on the green leg rest, his belt undone and his hands behind his head.

My lips twitch, for I want to say something that will make him uncomfortable after what I went through in his lesson yesterday. Instead, I keep it superficial. "I see you're working hard again." Zildryss moves to the back of my neck and plays under my hair.

Aymar's eyes open a crack, and his mouth turns up at the sides. "I was wondering when you two were going to turn up." Slowly, he rises to his feet and lazily yanks at his belt to secure it under his large stomach. "So, have either of you acted on your love interest today?"

Even though his voice is playful, I can't help glaring.

A blush colors Eir's cheeks. "Yes. I went to meet up with him today to see if what I feel is true."

Aymar's face lights with excitement. "Wonderful!"

As he turns to me, I meet his gaze by crossing my arms and tapping a foot with annoyance, and I answer with snark. "You know mine was a farce—a nonexistent person. So you know the answer." My glare tightens when the light elf chuckles, placing a hand on my shoulder. I shake it off.

He rubs his shoulder with the rejected hand. "Oh, Kara. Relax. We can't help what our hearts want."

"Whatever! Are we going to do this lesson or not?"

Zildryss pulls at my hair at the top of my neck, and I wince as annoyance fuels my anger. I ignore him. I'm not in the mood for his playfulness even though he's adorable.

The magic teacher laughs. "Of course, of course. Let us start our lesson." He claps his hands and rubs them together. "And what shall we work on today?" His question is rhetorical.

The little dragon continues to play under my hair, pulling on strands until they hurt.

I rub my scalp, trying to work away the discomfort. "Ow. Be careful, little guy. You're going to pull my hair right from my scalp."

A rare frown creases Aymar's face. "What're you talking about? You sound like you're going mad."

Zildryss releases my hair, and his smooth scales brush against my skin as he weaves around my neck to the front. His lilac face appears on my right, and he conducts his usual behavior, licking one eye then the other, his vision fixed on Aymar.

The light elf's jaw drops, catching sight of Zildryss sitting on my shoulder. "What the—" For the first time, Aymar seems at a loss for words. "Where did the dragon come from?" His wide eyes match the panic in his voice.

Confused by his panic, I ask, "What's the problem?"

Zildryss remains focused on the light elf, his tongue flicking from eye to eye. If what Elaith said is true, the little dragon is clearing his third eye. Yet I don't know why he's fixed so intently on Aymar. Even stranger, the more Zildryss stares at the elf, the more the teacher is panicking.

Eir stands next to me and rubs Zildryss's cheek with the back of a finger. She looks just as confused as I feel. "What's the matter? He's just a tiny little creature. He seems harmless and quite fond of the large dragons."

Aymar's face pales, and I embrace his shoulders to steady him before he passes out.

The light elf flinches. "Is that a long-mouthed guardian?"

I tighten my grip so that he won't fall to the ground. "Yes. Apparently."

Offering more support, Eir braces him on his other side. "Why?"

Zildryss coughs, projecting a large puff of smoke that billows around Aymar's face. The volume is impressive for such a small dragon.

The smoke hides the panic building in the elf's widening eyes.

Pushing aside my annoyance from yesterday, I muster some empathy. "Don't stress. It's just a little smoke that pretty much every dragon can ma—"

The smoke starts to clear, stripping my words with it. I drop my arm from his shoulders and back away. The elf's face thins before my eyes. The blue irises swirl and deepen in color until they are almost black. His blond hair lengthens to the shoulders, the color deepening until it's as black as Odin's ravens. Every pore of our light magic teacher transforms before our eyes into a completely different person.

Retreating, I almost stumble, struggling to speak. "Loki!"

Zildryss slaps his tail against the back of my neck, helping me out of my stupor, and I dive to clasp the god's wrists firmly. Eir calls to the dangling vines with her magic and wraps Loki's wrists securely several times, sealing the restraint with magic. Still coming to grips with this new reality, I somehow manage to clasp his bonds while Eir works on securing his ankles. The confusion on her face reflects my own.

The shock proves too hard to wipe away. He can't have tricked me again. He just can't. I thought it would have been Elaith if anybody on Alfheim.

"Oh, Vanir! What is going on?" I ask.

Eir shakes her head, her face solemn. "By the way, I've added magic to these bindings to stop you shapeshifting."

"Ooh. That's quite a talent you have. Did you learn that in a book?" Loki asks, snarky.

Tugging at the bindings around his wrists, I'm having trouble processing just how thin these arms are compared to the light elf, Aymar's. Ignoring his taunting of Eir, I ask, "Was it you the whole time?"

A broad, cheeky smile peers at me over his shoulder. "Of course."

The sudden urge to slap the deceptive god is hard

to control. Flashes of every single meeting with the elf Aymar go through my mind.

"Does Freyr know?" I ask.

Loki laughs, which drives my anger, twisting that embedded knife deeper in my stomach and winding me up more tightly.

Loki tosses his head back as though searching the sky for a reprieve. "Oh, please. As if that lovesick puppy would know anything."

Eir finishes restraining his feet and securing the vines with magic. "But he knew you as a magic teacher."

Loki lowers his gaze. "Well, of course. I was the spitting image of the magic teacher—the real magic teacher," he adds at the last second.

"What do you mean?" I stumble over my words, tackling a rising dread. "What happened to the real magic teacher?" I bite my bottom lip.

"Pfft!" Loki rolls his head. "Oh, don't stress. He's safe."

Ignoring the condescension, Eir asks, "Then where is he?"

The mischievous god rolls his eyes. "The way you two are acting, you would think I'm the evilest person in the world." Nonchalantly, he adds, "He's tied up somewhere in the bushes."

"Show us," I demand.

Clasping Loki's arms tightly, we let him lead us. Eventually, he brings us to a little spot enclosed in vines and leaves creating a sheltered area. In the center, a disheveled, slightly skinnier light elf than Loki's Aymar is bound and gagged in a corner. A strong smell of feces leaks out of the opening.

I retch and hold my spare hand over my nose. "Oh. Loki, that's disgusting! What have you done to the poor guy?"

"Nothing that can't be cleaned up. I have been feeding him—quite a bit, really. But he has lost a little weight. He's unquestionably a glutton."

Eir mutters something under her breath. The place cleans up, and the light elf's bindings and gag are released.

Slowly climbing to his feet, the real Aymar scrutinizes Loki. "And you wonder why the light elves don't like you. Freyr will hear about this."

"Yeah, yeah," Loki says sarcastically. "I'm already in deep trouble." He turns to me and smiles sweetly. "Nice to see you finally caught me, Kara. Although it isn't fair. You had a little helper." He scowls at the dragon still sitting on my shoulder.

Chapter Twenty-Three

Zildryss clings to the vines draped over the top of the hall, hanging from his talons or playfully jumping from vine to vine. Occasionally he pauses, his gaze traveling from Loki to Freyr, then Eir and myself, his tongue lashing one eye then the other.

The elven mess hall was empty, making it the best place to seat Loki on one of the benches, facing the table, his arms and legs still cuffed by the enchanted vines. Freyr stands over Loki, his arms crossed and legs splayed. A strange scowl covers his normally peaceful face. The loving god didn't take it well when he learned that Loki had kidnapped the village's magic teacher and replaced him. This happened right under his nose when he had been entrusted to protect us. A strange anger burns in his eyes. His cream tunic is spread open around the neck and scrunched oddly to one side under the rope belt.

"We have to leave the realm." The second the words are out of my mouth, I want to retract them. Sadness washes over Eir's face, instantly taking my thoughts to the auburn-haired elf she conjured as her love interest. Fighting off the burning anger from my experience with the exercise Loki made us do, I force myself to think of Eir. "Don't worry, Eir. You can come and visit him whenever you like after we're done delivering Loki."

She laces a loose strand of long brown hair behind her ear. "I don't know, Kara. I like being friends with you, but it's pretty hectic. Rarely is there time to visit other realms."

Picking a fallen leaf off her gown, I toss it aside. "I always appreciate your help and your company, but I'm not going to stop you from coming back. In fact, if that's what you want, I encourage it. You don't have to be by my side whenever I'm defending Asgard."

"And you think I'm not going to defend Asgard when I can?" Her eyes flash with disappointment.

I squeeze her forearm. "No, I just don't want to sacrifice the feelings of your heart either."

As understanding returns to her eyes, Freyr joins us, his attention still on Loki. "I'll watch him while you gather your dragons and things."

"Are you sure?" I ask.

He nods and runs a hand through his shoulder-length blond hair. "It's the least I can do after my failure. I promised Thor and Freya I'd protect you."

"It's not your fault. He's tricked us many times." Eir looks at the little dragon still swinging from the vines and smiles. "If it weren't for Zildryss, we probably still wouldn't know."

Some of the disappointment leaves his face. "In any case, it's still the least I can do." His face lightens. "Although I did manage to prevent Surt and his minions from entering our realm. You certainly managed to annoy him. He wasn't even interested in me, and I'm Freya's brother." He shakes his head.

ELAN AND NAGA are lying behind the cottage, which saves us having to look for them. After collecting our few things, we meet Freyr back in the hall.

Eir squeezes Freyr's hand. "Thank you for your hospitality. We had a lovely stay and will remember your kindness."

"You're more than welcome to return. Although I have failed in protecting you from the deceiver"—his eyes narrow on Loki, who grins in return—"I'm glad you enjoyed your visit."

I sling my quiver over my shoulder and climb onto Elan's back.

With the help of the real Aymar, Freyr loosens the restraints around Loki's feet and magically lifts him onto Elan's back behind me. Aymar then secures the vine from Loki's feet around his waist and attaches it to the saddle.

You know, I could just hang him from my talons. That would save all this effort. Elan grins, showing off her extensive array of teeth, and the elves circling us take a step back, their focus on the terrifying golden creature.

I can't help chuckling at their reaction. "It's all right. She's smiling."

A unified look of understanding crosses the elves' faces as their tension visibly melts away.

I rub under a scale in front of the saddle and answer her suggestion. "As much as I enjoy the thought, I think we should be civilized and let him ride on your back."

She harrumphs, stomping her feet. *Aw! You're such a spoilsport.*

As the peaceful god stares up at us, the frown lines on his face look strange. "It's sad to see you two go. You're leaving so soon, and I didn't get to spend as much time with you as I would've liked."

My heart softens. I was critical of this god when I

first saw him, judging him because of his open sexuality. Yet now, my heart warms at knowing he had our best interests in mind.

"You can thank Zildryss for finding Loki," I say. "He has brought our stay to a close early—although I can't deny that I'm looking forward to being allowed back into Asgard."

Freyr glances briefly at Zildryss, swinging like a little kid from the vines. "I'm glad you met the little long-mouthed guardian. Even though they are tiny, they're extremely wise and capable of powerful magic."

As though he knows we're talking about him, Zildryss swings from the vines and flips the right way up, gliding to Eir's shoulder and rubbing against her face. The sadness of leaving the realm evaporates for a moment, and a soft smile lightens her features, highlighting her beauty. Zildryss settles on her neck and rests his head on his front talons. Eir's attention returns to the crowd gathered to see us off, stopping when she spots a tall elf, his auburn hair glistening in the sun shining through the trees.

My heart weeps for her as sadness returns to her smile. She waves her fingers at him, and he blows her a kiss.

My thoughts are interrupted as Freyr continues, "I sent word back to Thor, telling him to inform Odin that you've captured Loki and you're on your way back to Asgard." He glares at the devious god bound to Elan's saddle. "I'm glad to see my real magic teacher back in business, albeit a little shaken."

Loki straightens behind me. "I didn't harm a hair on his head."

Ignoring Loki's comment, Freyr returns his gaze to me. "Safe travels. Thor is waiting for you, and you're allowed back in Asgard without any punishment."

A massive weight lifts off my shoulders—a pressure I'd carried ever since Ratatoskr delivered the dreadful news. "Thank you for your hospitality, Freyr. I will tell your sister that you have looked after us."

"Please do. Otherwise, I'll never hear the end of it." The panic in his voice almost makes me smile— tiny little sensual Freya has her brother under her thumb. "And please tell Thor the same. I promised him as much."

"I will."

Elan and Naga push into the air and fly straight to the Yggdrasil, diving into the hole in the trunk and back to Asgard. The flight is much shorter than traveling from Muspelheim, not to mention the scenery being much more pleasant.

The change of trees and lakes to jutting rocks and

mountains is a strangely pleasant one. Even though the landscape of Alfheim is much prettier than Asgard's, the latter is my home, and nothing else is like the sense of peace I get every time I arrive home after a long trip.

The second we land outside Odin's palace, we are greeted by Birger and Gorm. Gorm's broad clefted chin juts out in determination as they temporarily leave their posts, quickly running down the court-yard to help secure Loki.

Elan's voice pierces my thoughts. *Thor!*

Soon, Thor appears at the front steps, gliding down them two at a time while Birger and Gorm yank the mischievous god off Elan's lowered back. Still sitting on Naga's back, Eir secures the loosened vines around Loki and ties them around the two guards' waists, making Loki's escape impossible. The brief shock that crosses the guards' faces before they realize what Eir was doing is priceless. Only a moment is wasted before Birger and Gorm lead Loki to the palace dungeons.

Thor chuckles, also recovering from the unex-pected magic Eir performs. "Good job. You've done well. Odin has allowed you back into Asgard, Kara. Although it pains me to say this, don't expect the same treatment as before." He slaps me on the back, and my body lurches forward.

The little dragon flies off Eir's shoulder and lands on mine, snarling at Thor.

"It's okay, little guy." I scratch him under the chin, and he retracts his teeth. "He looks rough and slaps hard, but it's meant in a friendly way." Zildryss's tongue flicks from eye to eye, never leaving Thor.

As though insecure under the little dragon's scrutinizing stare, Thor chuckles, his attention on Zildryss. "And what do we have here?"

I run a finger over his soft, membranous wings. "This is the little guy that revealed Loki to us. Loki was in shape-shifting form again, and this guy stripped him of that." I raise an eyebrow at the god of thunder. "He's powerful. Don't take his size for granted."

Thor points his finger at the dragon, and Zildryss bites him on the fingertip.

Thor yanks his finger away and shakes it. "Ow! Nasty!" His next chuckle is apprehensive. "Okay, okay, little guy. I will take you seriously."

Zildryss smirks then flies to Thor's shoulder, worming his way through the god's bushy auburn beard before climbing through his hair and over his head. Thor chuckles nervously while swiping large hands toward the dragon. "Okay, little guy. That tickles. Please get out of my hair."

The little dragon climbs into Thor's hand, wrapping his talons around his large fingers, and stares up at the big god.

A thump sounds as Eir climbs off Naga. "I think he likes you."

Thor lifts a bushy red eyebrow. "Then why did he bite me?"

I chuckle. "Because you're annoying."

Thor nudges me on my upper arm, lurching me sideways. "We're about to secure Fenrir again, under the ruse that he has a chance to prove his strength. Do you want to come?"

"I guess I should come and see if it works." I glance at Eir, who looks as unenthusiastic as I feel.

I knew Fenrir as a pup, and the thought of him turning aggressive is disturbing—whether because of his father's capture or his going through his teenage years. He was such a cute pup.

Thor leads us down to the gods' gathering spot in front of Fenrir. Odin leads the group, and Fenrir snarls at the gods surrounding him. A large, heavy chain is slung between the gods, distributing the weight.

Fenrir growls. "That chain is thicker than your arms. What do you expect to do with that?"

Odin struggles under the weight yet still manages to lift it higher for the giant hound to see. "What's wrong, Fenrir? If you're too scared to see if you can break it, then the title of the strongest will have to go to the gods, and you can remain a weak dog."

The lips draw back, exposing Fenrir's teeth. "You know that's not true."

"Then prove it," Odin taunts.

The hesitation flashing across Fenrir's face washes away, and he lowers to his stomach, the muscles in his neck bulging as he allows the gods to wrap the thick chain around his neck.

The gods secure the chain, fixing the end to a large boulder. Slowly, Fenrir rises to his feet and pushes against the restraint. Every muscle in his legs and torso pull tightly against the chain. The hound grinds his teeth, straining every muscle, inching a little farther with each breath. Eventually, a loud crack reverberates off the side of the boulder as the chain snaps, and Fenrir stumbles and straightens himself. Panting, he looks at me. "What is she doing here?"

Backing away, I bite my bottom lip, taken aback by his comment.

In the blink of an eye, Tyr is by Fenrir's side, stroking the large hound's nose. "Now, Fenrir. It's Kara… our Valkyrie friend."

Fenrir snarls. "She's the one that got my father into all this trouble in the first place." He thumps a paw angrily on the ground. "Why's she back? Is my father captured?" His eyes find Thor then Odin. "I thought she was banished."

"She was banished," Odin says stiffly, his gaze cold as it lands on me, and he raises his chin. "I've let her back in because she's recaptured your father. It's where he deserves to be."

Fenrir sneers, jumping over Tyr and edging toward Odin, eyeing me sideways.

Tyr darts around the large body to the front, holding his hands out. "Stop, Fenrir."

Fixing my gaze right back at him, I cross my arms. "Your father has done bad things. He's not chained under dripping venom anymore, but he's secured. This is what he deserves after all the pain he has caused Asgard."

Fenrir's hackles rise, and he stalks forward, his head lowered, ready to attack.

Tyr waves his hands in front of Fenrir, trying to clasp the hound's attention. "We're going to look after him this time. He won't experience pain like last time, I promise, but he will be secured."

Fenrir's hackles slowly lower, and he sits on the ground. He glares at Odin then at me. "This better be true, or else." His head rises from his stalking stance, his voice smug. "I've proven I'm stronger than these gods."

I nod, not knowing what to say, and back away.

Feeling Eir by my side and Zildryss on my shoulder, I head toward Elan, who's waiting over the hill.

Thor notices my retreat and follows. "Kara, I think you need to take on a mission." He flicks his fur coat behind himself and places his fists on his hips.

I stare at him, wide-eyed, and I'm almost ashamed at the whine in my voice. "What do you mean? I just got back."

"To protect Asgard, we have to take action."

I frown.

"You saw how Fenrir acted. Now that Loki is secured, we need to work on the children. Undoubtedly, Jormungandr is turning in Midgard's waters, and Hel is plotting something. But the first immediate threat is Fenrir."

I cross my arms, unconvinced.

"Didn't you see he has it in for Odin? If anything happens to Loki, he's going to cause some trouble. I can see it in his eyes. I've known him since he was a little hound. He was adorable when Tyr and I brought him to Asgard. Now, his sweetness is gone, and only vengeance lies in his eyes."

Uncrossing my arms, I stand straight. "And where are we meant to go?"

Thor fiddles with his belt. "Svartalfheim."

The suggestion nearly makes me stumble backward in shock. "Why there? Why the land of the dwarfs? None of his children are there."

"Haven't you heard that they make a lot of fantastic equipment? They made my hammer, my belt, Odin's scepter, and many other useful artifacts. I've heard they can make a fine rope stronger than any chain we have made on Asgard, but it looks like thin fabric. We need to ask them to make it for us. And I need you to come with me."

THE END

Stay Tuned. Book 5 in Thor's Dragon Rider series will be released before mid 2021.

If you enjoyed Hoodwinked, please take a few minutes and leave a review on Amazon. Thank you. Reviews help authors.

ACKNOWLEDGMENTS

Thank you to all of the creators of literature and websites who have spent time writing about Norse Mythology. Even though at times there has been contradicting information, it has been an interesting study. After all, of course a goat produces mead, and a dragon gnaws at the roots of the Yggdrasil, unhindered, threatening the existence of the nine realms attached to the world tree. Plus, there are many other "believable" tales told.

Norse mythology is such an impressive set of tales that I have incorporated some and invented others to create Kara and Elan's story.

I am touched by the enormous amount of support I have received from my immediate family. My husband has been a helpful first reader and, at times, been an excellent motivator, with hints of ideas to help me through the blanks. The support from my three sons has also been overwhelming. They have spent years putting up with my head in the clouds, thinking about the next plot twist or story, along with many hours spent working on my books and keeping in touch with my readers.

A big thank you to my extended family, who support me being a book enthusiast.

A huge thank you to my editor, Kelly Reed, her editing and writing tips, and my proofreader, Laura K., for picking up the things we missed.

Thank you to all of my readers who have loved my work, and continue to read my stories.

BOOKS BY KATRINA COPE

Pre-Teen Books

The Sanctum Series

JAYDEN'S CYBERMOUNTAIN

SCARLET'S ESCAPE

TAYLOR'S PLIGHT

ERIC & THE BLACK AXES

ADRIANNA'S SURGE

~~~~~

Young Adult Urban Fantasy

Afterlife Series

FLEDGLING

THE TAKING

ANGELIC RETRIBUTION

DIVIDED PATHS

TRUTH HUNTER

Afterlife Novelette

THE GATEKEEPER

~~~~~

Young Adult Urban Paranormal Fantasy

<u>Supernatural Evolvement Series</u>

(Associated with the Afterlife Series)

WITCH'S LEGACY (Prequel)

AALIYAH

~~~~~

Young Adult Norse Mythology Fantasy

<u>Valkyrie Academy Dragon Alliance</u>

MARKED

CHOSEN

VANISHED

SCORNED

INFLICTED

EMPOWERED

AMBUSHED

WARNED

ABDUCTED

BESIEGED

DECEIVED

<u>Thor's Dragon Rider</u>

SAFEGUARD

PURSUIT

ENTRAPMENT
~~~~~

HOODWINKED

More to come

ABOUT THE AUTHOR

Katrina is a best-selling author of young adult fantasy and middle grade/tween novels. Her novels incorporate action, heart and an intriguing plot.

She resides in Queensland, Australia. Her three teenage boys and husband for over twenty years treat her like a princess. Unfortunately though, this princess still has to do domestic chores.

From a very young age, she has been a very creative person and has spent many years travelling the world and observing many different personalities and cultures. Her favourite personalities have been the strange ones, yet the ones under the radar also hold a place in her heart.

Katrina's online home is at www.katrinacopebooks.com

You can connect with Katrina on:

Facebook Group

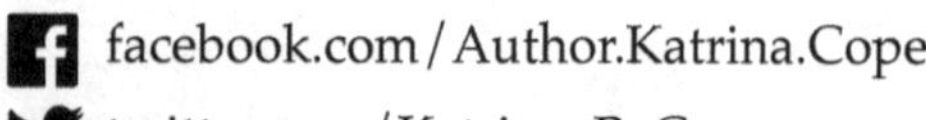

facebook.com/Author.Katrina.Cope

twitter.com/Katrina_R_Cope

instagram.com/katrina_cope_author

pinterest.com/katrinacope56

bookbub.com/profile/katrina-cope

www.ingramcontent.com/pod-product-compliance
Lightning Source LLC
Chambersburg PA
CBHW020142120726

47903CB00007B/2377